Praise for *Enough to Lose*

"This book is the best thing I've read lately, with its dead-on depictions of rural life, both beautiful and heart-wrenching. With its floods, guns, car wrecks, dangerous bridges, bars that 'stay open out of habit,' there's a lot at stake here. Deeren is a keen observer of what age, poverty, and bad luck can do to a body: forty-five is, he says, 'the age where you'll have enough to lose that you'll lose yourself in the process of trying to hold onto everything.' Some of his characters live so close to the edge that the failure of a freezer might mean going hungry, while others move closer to the edge to feel alive or to grieve fully. If you say these characters are stubbornly behind the times, it's because they are not buying what America is offering them—they are holding out for something better and more meaningful. They have tasted the sweetness of romantic love, they have felt in their bones the elegance of a deer crossing a river. Deeren's strong, sure, authentic voice sings the songs of Michigan, and you should listen."

—Bonnie Jo Campbell, author of
Mothers, Tell Your Daughters

"*Enough to Lose* is compulsively readable. Like Denis Johnson, Richard Russo, and Daniel Woodrell, Deeren's stories reflect the often brutal reality of working-class, rural life, punctuated by moments of beauty and brilliance. Filled with nuance, *Enough to Lose* prompts readers to think about the humanity of those who might have experiences vastly different than their own."

—Donald Quist, author of *For Other Ghosts*
and *To Those Bounded*

"A barn burner of love and longing, *Enough to Lose* delivers gut-punch stories over and over, each one studded with fierce insights about class and family and rural living and rendered in tender, electric prose."

—Karen Tucker, author of *Bewilderness*

T0054651

"RS Deeren's riveting first collection, written in the vein of Jim Harrison, Bonnie Jo Campbell, and Breece D'J Pancake, spotlights rural Michigan in all of its variegated beauty and pathos. Deeren's years as a substitute teacher, landscaper, and lumberjack perhaps contributed to the visceral quality of this fresh new work. The people in these stories often struggle to make it, but the struggle here feels real and true. Deeren's unflinching yet empathetic attention fosters a human connection between the reader and the characters in these stories that outpaces the heartbreak and renders this book a must-read."

—Kelly Fordon, author of *I Have the Answer*
(Wayne State University Press)

"Reader, be prepared, as you open *Enough to Lose*, RS Deeren's wonderful debut short story collection, to enter a world—in this case the thumb of Michigan—that's as vividly and evocatively detailed as any in contemporary fiction."

—Larry Watson, author of *Montana 1948*,
Let Him Go, and other novels

ENOUGH
TO
LOSE

Made in Michigan Writers Series

General Editors

Michael Delp, Interlochen Center for the Arts
M. L. Liebler, Wayne State University

A complete listing of the books in this series can
be found online at wsupress.wayne.edu.

ENOUGH TO LOSE

Stories by
RS DEEREN

WAYNE STATE UNIVERSITY PRESS
DETROIT

ISBN 9780814350409 (paperback)
ISBN 9780814350416 (e-book)

Library of Congress Control Number: 2023931600

Cover image © Dan Dunkley / Offset.com. Cover design by Laura Klynstra.

Publication of this book was made possible by a generous gift from The Meijer Foundation.

Wayne State University Press rests on Waawiyaataanong, also referred to as Detroit, the ancestral and contemporary homeland of the Three Fires Confederacy. These sovereign lands were granted by the Ojibwe, Odawa, Potawatomi, and Wyandot Nations, in 1807, through the Treaty of Detroit. Wayne State University Press affirms Indigenous sovereignty and honors all tribes with a connection to Detroit. With our Native neighbors, the press works to advance educational equity and promote a better future for the earth and all people.

Wayne State University Press
Leonard N. Simons Building
4809 Woodward Avenue
Detroit, Michigan 48201-1309

Visit us online at wsupress.wayne.edu.

For Janel, Mom, Dad, and Home

Contents

THE MIRROR

The river crested ten feet too late, so there'd be no saving the house. FEMA had designated the land between the river and the house Zone A with no Base Flood Elevations determined, which meant that, in the grand plan of putting houses where people wanted them but not necessarily where nature would tolerate them, it was legal from the county's perspective to build. "Go ahead," said the surveyor. "At home on the banks of a lazy river," said the Realtor. "You've always wanted your own place to fish," Jackie Chuberts said to her husband, Chubs. It was all she needed to say to convince him to buy.

From an insurance perspective, no BFE meant no flood coverage, which meant no claim, which meant that the new carpeting the Chuberts had just laid, the pots and pans from the wedding registry, and even her mother's ottoman—the same one Jackie used to sit on as a kid when she'd listen to the Tigers' game on the radio while her mother drew a diamond on a napkin to track each hit—were all nothing more than memories floating downriver waiting to be collected by scavengers and scrapped.

That is, after the damn water receded.

———

Earlier that week, the weatherman said to expect some light rain across Michigan's Thumb region, with more severe storms drifting to the south and west over Detroit, Flint, and Saginaw. That was just dandy, Jackie thought. She could finish painting the walls in the second bedroom, then start on the molding. Chubs could do the same in the main bedroom. With twenty acres of land, mostly ash and cedar woods, they had plenty of work to do outside, and, with a thirty-year mortgage, more than plenty of time to get it done.

Thirty years, Jackie thought as she finished outlining the doorframe in eggshell white paint. They'd own this corner of paradise outright by summer 2016. She set the brush on the rim of the can and wiped sweat from her forehead. That year seemed unreal, too far away to fathom. She heard her husband across the hall, grunting while he painted.

"How's it going in there?" she called.

"Good," he replied. "We need a higher step ladder. You good in there?"

Jackie looked over the outlining she'd done. The room was the perfect size for a child's bedroom. The neutral color on the wall could be easily coated over with whatever color a teenager might want. Then, once she and Chubs were empty nesters, it could become a hobby room. She'd always loved pressing flowers. Maybe by then they would be painting these same walls a different color, anxiously awaiting a visit from their daughter. Or son. Jackie placed a hand on her belly. When to tell her husband? The last time, they'd gotten too excited, told too many friends and family, which made it not taking even harder to handle. This time, it would be best to be sure before telling anyone. Including Chubs.

"Doing fine," she said. "I wish it would stop raining, though." She poured some paint into a roller pan and began the first coat.

That weatherman sure didn't know what he was talking about. For days it had rained in sheets. In the middle of the first night, the two had decided to head to town to buy burlap sacks to fill with earth. They would barricade the doors, just in case, and continue fixing the interior of the house while the rain passed over. But news had come over the radio on the second day saying that Caro had lost power and all local businesses had boarded themselves up.

Fine, Jackie thought. We're off the village grid and still have power. The bathroom floor tiles need regrouting, and I can paint the kitchen.

She knew Chubs was a firm believer that as long as they had a roof over their heads, they would turn out fine. He could start his new job next week and eventually they would have life down to a cozy routine, living fence to fence in the city a distant memory. Let it rain, she decided. We're safe in here.

They had eaten eggs and toast for dinner on the second and third nights, listening to the weather forecast. The storm had caught moisture up from the Gulf and now Canada was breathing down on it (the weatherman's words). Fed by the winds, it now stretched from Michigan's sunrise side, over Lake Michigan, and up to the Lake Superior coast of Wisconsin; the storm that had been predicted to run its course in a single day had lingered, then stalled.

———

On the fourth morning, Jackie heard the water first, splashing down from the ceiling of the master bedroom. She walked down the hall, past the bathroom where Chubs was hanging the antique mirror his grandmother had given him. At the door to the bedroom, the carpet squished under her feet.

"Chubs," she yelled. "Chubs, rain's coming in." Across the room, a pool of water was growing on the floor under the window. Jackie knew she wouldn't be able to do anything. A finger in a dike is just a front row seat to something horrible. Fifteen yards outside the window, planks of wood, deck chairs, and what looked like the top half of a toolshed floated downriver.

Chubs was in the middle of balancing the mirror. Jackie ran to the kitchen and grabbed a new soup pot. She threw it under the drip, creating a water-on-metal *ping ping ping*.

"Chubs!"

"Yeah, Jak, I hear you. One second."

That afternoon, the seals on most of the plumbing gave way, and Chubs spent the ensuing hours under the bathroom and kitchen sinks with a flashlight between his teeth and water dripping on his face. Jackie paced through the rooms of the house with the pots and pans, zeroing in on the drops coming through the roof that the Realtor's inspector had marked as "satisfactory" on his official report. The pots filled every half hour, and she began a cycle of emptying them into the bathtub. The tar-yellow water pooled, draining slower than it should have. She'd spent her entire life with city water and never knew a house with a septic field instead of sewage lines, so when the rain began to fall, it felt like nature's attack on the homestead started there.

"We weren't supposed to get this much rain, were we?" Jackie crouched next to Chubs and passed him half of a peanut butter sandwich.

"That doesn't matter," he said. "It's falling anyway."

In the dark, a convoy of three pickup trucks pulled up the mud driveway, their fog beams bleeding orange against the wall of rain. Jackie tapped her husband's heel with her toe and leaned over the kitchen sink.

"Someone's here," she said. Through the drain, she watched Chubs wrap duct tape around the drainpipe's end. Plumbing was not his strong suit. The flashlight was wedged under his chin, and he was trying to peel a length of tape with his teeth.

The driver of the first truck got out and ran up the porch. He pounded and pounded on the door.

"Hey!" he said. "Open up."

Had it not been for the weather, Jackie wouldn't have let him in so quickly. She remembered her mother telling her not to talk to strangers when she was little, could hear her say to never let men she barely knew into her home. But for God's sake, the man had to all but swim the few yards to get to the door, and the roof had more leaks than she had pans. The tub was half-filled with grime, and Chubs was still screwing with the kitchen sink. The voice of her mother was just going to have to shut it.

"What the heck are you doing out in this?" she said. She pulled a towel from the drawer.

The man ran it over his head and face. "Look, you don't know me. The name's Alton Southby. Al. Listen, this here storm ain't going anywhere soon. The Romain boys're out front. We're gonna get you folks somewhere dry."

"Who is it, Jackie?" Chubs said to the pipe drain.

"A neighbor," Jackie said. "Look, Mr. Southby—"

"Al."

"Fine," Jackie said. "Al. What are you talking about?"

"Jesus Christ," Chubs said.

A new leak in the roof poured through the drain. Jackie grabbed the towel from Al and tossed it to Chubs who stuffed it into the bottom of the sink.

Jackie fought a fuzzy dizziness around her temples. The drips plopped and rang in the pans and the rain pelted the new double-paned windows. When she and Chubs had toured the property for the first time, the summer was still in the middle of a drought. She had walked down to the riverbank. This far up, the Cass River was hardly more than a stream, their Realtor had said. A narrow line of water ran along the cracked riverbed, smelling of fish and warm dead leaves. Jackie loved that smell, but she loved it in its own world, sixty yards away from her kitchen sink. Now, as she hovered over her husband, with a stranger soaking the floor inside her front door, she felt the smell rotting the little hairs inside her nostrils.

"You don't have time for this," Al said. "The river is rising. Grab what you can. Things that can survive a soaking. The boys got room in their beds."

Chubs climbed out from under the sink, holding a busted trap assembly in his hand.

"You got any kids?" Al asked.

"Excuse me?" Jackie felt herself go flush. It all felt like a violation—this rain, this stranger in her home and then in her thoughts.

"This is an evacuation, folks," Al said. "Kids first."

"No kids," Chubs answered.

"Alright," Al said, "Let's get to it."

Through the window, Jackie saw one of the trucks flashing its high beams. A horn blared. This is what she'd call a sign—from God or some other interested party, it didn't matter to her. She believed Chubs recognized good advice when he heard it, and she did her damnedest to get him to listen as often as possible.

In a mad dash between the house and the trucks, they managed armfuls of clothing, canned food, and linens from the hallway closet. There hadn't been time for Al to introduce the two other men with him. All Jackie knew was what Al had told her: they were brothers, neighbors, ready to help. For a moment, when she was shoving sweaters into the back of one of their trucks, she thought maybe this was a con. Maybe these men were vultures taking advantage of the storm, pretending to be good Samaritans but ready to rob her and Chubs blind. What the team was removing from the house, though, wasn't anything worth stealing, and no matter how badly she wanted to think this storm was a bad dream, it was real, and it was getting worse.

The rain fell steady and Al promised a hot shower at his place some ten miles up the road, safely perched at the top of the river valley. Tired, drenched, and shaking from adrenaline, the Romain brothers stuffed themselves into the trucks and waited for the Chuberts and Al to make a final pass inside. In the bathroom, Chubs wrangled with the mirror he'd hung.

"Whoa, buddy," Al said, "Ain't got room for that."

"We'll make room," Chubs said. "I love this mirror."

"It's a mirror," Al said. "I got one in my bathroom you can use."

"It was his grandmother's," Jackie said. She had a laundry basket full of groceries. Corn Flakes, red beans, and canned peas. "She raised him." Al looked at her. She at her husband. Chubs at his reflection in the mirror.

"It's all we've got left of her," Chubs said. "This is our home, and she's part of it."

"He promised her he'd move her out of the city," Jackie said.

"Shit." Al looked around. "What about the bedroom? We can wrap it up on the bed." Chubs shook his head. "Hey man, it's the best we can do. It's got a better chance with some kind of roof over it than sitting in the storm."

The three of them stared out from the mirror, wet and dirty. A line of water spilled onto the glass from a crack in the ceiling.

"If we have to," Chubs said.

Outside, they waded toward the trucks. The water had drowned the tomato garden and only the red tip of a garden gnome's hat pointed out from the water. As the trucks began up the driveway, a wave of water pushed into their grills.

"Whoa, baby," Al said. He held onto the wheel, struggling and failing to keep it straight. The water didn't stop. He stuck his head out the window for a better view. There was no road to see, just more river. "Christ," he said, "we're washed in."

"There's the barn," Jackie said from the backseat. "At the back of the property. Our car's parked by it."

The pole barn was fifty yards behind the house and a good two hundred from where the river should have been. It was nothing more than steel siding, a roof, and a dirt floor. The convoy inched their way up to it, parking as far away from the river as possible.

When they had finally collapsed in the barn, everyone was too exhausted for anything more than pleasantries. They exchanged names then ate canned vegetables in silence. The Romains were twins, Robert and Randall. Before Jackie had finished eating, both were already stretched out on the floor, falling asleep. Al wasn't too far behind them.

Jackie and Chubs couldn't close their eyes. That night, while Al and the brothers slept, Jackie and Chubs sat by the door, listening to the storm. The barn had an old cast-iron woodstove in the back corner that the Romains had tried to light, but when they opened it, ashy water flowed out.

She pulled his head to her chest, and he curled his arm around her waist. He squeezed her and she thought, *Tell him now.*

"What's that noise?" Chubs asked.

Through the gravelly pour of rain on the barn roof and the moaning of tree roots pressed against the force of the river, a loud sucking came from the house, like a small child trying to pull their boot from the mud. Slow, waterlogged.

"That sounded expensive," she said.

"Too expensive," he said.

Leaning outside the door, they couldn't see anything but the outline of the house. Water lapped at the bottom of the vinyl siding. A few times, a loud crack came from one of the main supports.

———

The next morning, Jackie tried to start a fire. The roof had held throughout the night, but all the rain had continued to flood the chimney. The smell of wet soot hung over the smell of wet men. There wasn't much in the barn left behind by the original owner. Only stacks of wood and newspapers. The newest of these papers, which Chubs used as a pillow, was already twenty years old.

Jackie sidestepped the men sleeping on swathes of old newsprint. Peeking through the crack of the door, everything was brighter. To the south beyond the tree line, she swore to God, was a patch of blue sky. Everything still smelled like fish, but now there was some wind, a sign, she hoped, that the storm was moving out over Lake Huron, and would become Canada's problem.

The other men snored and groaned. Al slept propped against the edge of an empty workbench. Jackie noticed for the first time how old he looked. He had glasses with small round lenses. It was the kind of thing she would have noticed when she wasn't evacuating herself and all she could carry from a house with a Swiss cheese roof. The night before, Al had been so forward, so ready to act just to get her and her husband away from the river. Action, she figured, overruled age in a way that nothing else could. Fear came close. Love, too. Now, with his arms folded over his chest, he seemed to her to have never known any other pose.

She tiptoed back to her husband.

"Chubs," she said. Chubs's eyeballs darted beneath his eyelids. She knelt on a paper, circa 1954, and shook her husband awake.

"I wasn't sleeping," he said. "I'm up." He closed his eyes again.

"Honey, it's not raining that bad. I think it's over." Chubs opened his eyes and cleared his throat.

"Goddamnit," he said. "What a night. What a mess." He leaned forward on his knees and looked down at a *Detroit Free Press* sports page. Two girls cheering at Tiger Stadium on opening day. "What's the damage?"

"Don't know," Jackie said. She put her arm around him. "The house is still there."

As the morning progressed, the men woke. Al came to the door where the Chuberts stood watching the rain.

"At least you can see a few yards," he said. He yawned, stretched, and patted them on the shoulders.

The Romains had busied themselves with replacing their wet newspapers with dry, bickering over where to place the fresh paper.

"Boys," Al said. "Say 'hi' to the new neighbors."

"Morning."

"Pleasure."

The Chuberts eked out smiles. Chubs quickly turned his attention back outside and toward the house.

"What now?" he said.

"We should eat something," Jackie said. She opened a box of cereal and began to pour out handfuls to the men. Outside, the road was still an extension of the river.

"Maybe we could get some more food from the house," Chubs said.

"You think that's the best idea?" Al asked.

"It's better than half a cup of cereal and canned veggies. We left the weather radio in there, too." He stuck his arm outside to feel the rain. "It's gotta be clearing up."

"Let's wait a while longer," Jackie said. She plopped down next to the twins and poured some Corn Flakes into her palm.

"I hate Corn Flakes," Randall said.

"You'd hate starving even more," Robert said.

The rain didn't get any worse as the day grew. At some points, Jackie even had an idea of where the sun was above the river and rain and clouds. Chubs spent most of his time at the barn door, fixated on the house. Between the two structures, large puddles swamped their yard. The river had risen to fully encircle the house, and water splashed onto the porch.

Over a lunch of dry cereal, Robert told Jackie how Al had rallied him and his brother to get here.

Al dug through the laundry basket of food, deciding on canned white potatoes.

"I just hope no one got lost in the flood," he said. He pulled out a pocketknife and went to work on the can.

"County bigwigs probably ain't got the slightest idea how bad it is out here," Randall said. He kicked at a pile of newspapers, chewing at his lips. He kicked another pile over and then another before plopping down to read an article detailing the grand opening of a drive-in theater.

"What about Caro?" Chubs asked. "Wouldn't they send somebody?"

Randall snorted at this but kept his nose in the paper.

"We're way outside the village limits," Robert said. "Technically we're closer to Cass City, and they're even less equipped to help." He poured cereal into his hand then passed the box around.

"The farther up in the Thumb you go," Robert said.

"The farther you get from certain comforts," Randall said.

"The county can't get here 'til the water levels fall," Al continued.

"So, we just have to wait?" Chubs asked.

Al shrugged. "That's just part of living here. You either get used to waiting or you learn to make do on your own."

Jackie knew the Thumb, or at least she'd studied its shape in the atlas she used to look at after Chubs went to sleep. Caro was almost one hundred miles from Detroit. North on I-75 to Michigan Highway 24, far beyond the stretch of suburban parking lots, rural farmland, and into the woods. Chubs had told her time and again that his grandmother had wanted this life for him. A wide-open life away from the noise of the city, where Chubs could become a real man, do some fishing, learn real hunting that was more than chasing around rabbits under an overpass with a hockey stick. *Simple*, his grandmother called it. For as long as Jackie knew Chubs, he'd always been focused on making his grandmother's dream a reality. She admired that drive. It made it easy to fall in love with him.

Still, none of them had ever lived outside of Detroit, and in the short time she and Chubs had owned the house, country living was anything but simple. Jackie knew that much.

But she didn't know the place like these men knew it; she saw that now. Beyond the house, on the far bank of the river, lengths of fallen tree trunks jammed along ones still standing, creating a wall the water rushed over in loud waves.

"You make it sound like some kind of deserted island," Chubs said.

"A peninsula on a peninsula," Al said. "Lots of water for folks to keep their backs to while keeping the rest of the world in front of them."

"At least we're out of the rain," Jackie said.

"It's bad," Randall said, "but it doesn't seem to be getting worse."

"That still keeps us at bad," Robert said.

—

"I'm sure I can make it to the house," Chubs said. He leaned on the doorjamb, kicking at the mud. Behind him, the group read old news and compared the prices of corn and soybeans across the decades.

"Chubs, don't," Jackie said. She looped her arm around his. She had spent the day fighting herself, hushing the voice inside her head that told her to tell Chubs she was pregnant. It would give him something other than the house to focus on, but it was still early, earlier than their first try.

"Jak, think of it," Chubs said. "All the photos we left, the rest of the food, Grandma's mirror. Did we even grab extra socks?"

They had not, in fact, grabbed any extra socks. Or underwear for that matter. The only things they'd managed to get in the scuffle were jeans and a couple sweatshirts. All of which hung around the barn trying their hardest to dry. Chubs hugged her. She felt his steady heartbeat, and a part of her agreed with him, but there was still way more inside of her that feared the water.

"Look at this," Randall said. "I found a write-up from when the Ark Church burned down." He pushed himself up and walked over to his brother who dozed on the floor. "Robert, you remember this, don't you?" He kicked his brother's foot.

"I'm trying to sleep," he said.

"You slept last night. C'mon, you'll like this little blast from the past." He crouched down and dangled the yellowed paper above Robert's face. "Our parents took us to Sunday school there until it went up in flames," Randall said.

"Thank God for that fire," Robert said. "The place was boring."

"I didn't think so," Randall said. "I mean, some of that stuff was pretty cool. Like people turning into salt." He pulled the paper away from his brother and reread.

"Or what about Noah?" Robert said.

Al rolled his eyes. "They rebuilt that place as soon as it burned," he said. "The quickest things to go up in this county are churches."

"And taxes!" the brothers added. The three men laughed and flipped through more papers.

"A building can disappear in a blink," Chubs said. He kept his gaze out across the water. "If there isn't someone around to do something about it, everything could be lost."

Jackie felt his breath deepen. She rubbed his back and kissed his cheek.

"Let's eat something," Jackie said. "What's on the menu, Al?"

"Looks like three cans of apple pie filling and two cans of fried onion topping," he said.

"That's it?" Jackie asked.

"We'll have to ration," Al continued. "Hey, Romains, that church ever teach you about fasting?"

Jackie stumbled to the basket, thinking that maybe Al was the type of guy who cracked jokes in times like these, a coping mechanism of some sort. The kind of thing that, if someone didn't know a person, they'd be quick to think the guy was something of an ass because, really, who lies about what kind of food is left when people are trapped in a pole barn and there is a flood where there hadn't been one mere days earlier? But Al wasn't lying. There was only pie filling and onions.

Hunger boiled in her chest and throat, coating her tongue with bile. So, this was it, she thought. No intimate moment to themselves when she could tell her husband the news. Just a dirt floor, three waterlogged strangers, and the rest of their food as good as gone. She cupped her hands over her face and ran her fingers along her eyebrows and temples, down to her jaw. This could be a good story to tell her child years from now, with the men becoming more waterlogged and the river turning to rapids as the story evolved through its retelling. Chubs could play the hero, wading through the current and returning with food. Jackie turned to the door, to her husband. But he wasn't there.

At the barn door Jackie yelled for her husband. He was already halfway to the house. The wind kicked up and Jackie heard tree branches crashing in the woods. Jackie began after him but stopped when her feet sank into the engorged earth, sucking and popping as she pulled them free. Al and the brothers were already at her side.

"Get back here, you idiot!" Jackie hollered. Chubs didn't turn around.

The water had risen in the night and was still falling with no place to go but to places it wasn't welcome. Like on the back porch.

Something was wedged against the back door. Now calf deep, Chubs froze, and in that split second, the current knocked him sideways.

Jackie gasped as she saw Chubs go under. He regained his footing.

The moment hit Jackie like a decade.

"Come back," Jackie screamed, stepping toward him only to have three sets of hands hold her back.

"What's that across the door?" Randall said.

"Is that a body?" Robert said.

Jackie nearly vomited at the idea of a body, someone upriver who had fallen into the drink and was gone, just like that.

Al squinted. "I think it's a deer."

Chubs climbed over the thing and kicked it away from the door. The brown mass churned in the current. It was a dead deer, its head lolling as it drifted in front of Jackie. When she turned back to the door, it was open, and Chubs was out of sight. Another moment of panic washed over her as she thought Chubs had fallen again.

"Henry Delaney Chuberts," she yelled. Water rushed into their house, carrying with it hunks of wood, lawn debris, and mud.

She saw Chubs then, in the kitchen window. He was running in and out of view, disappearing into the shadows deeper inside the house.

"What's he doing?" Robert said.

Jackie tried pulling free from the men, but their grips were firm, and her feet had sunk into the earth again.

Chubs opened the kitchen widow and punched out the screen. Cans flew from it, one after the other, plopping into the water. Some making it beyond where the river had crested. He leaned out of the window and yelled something, but Jackie couldn't make out what it was. He pointed at the cans.

"Food!" Al said. He ran back to the barn to retrieve the laundry basket.

"He's cleaning out what we couldn't get before," Randall said.

The twins high stepped their way toward the cans, tossing the closer ones back toward the barn where Al collected them. Chubs threw more cans. The twins locked arms like a short human chain so they could reach the ones that had landed in the water.

Jackie's chest heaved as she watched the cans shoot out of the dark window. This was insane. If she had only told Chubs they were pregnant again, no way he would have risked his life for a dozen cans of Jolly Green Giant.

"Mother of God," Al said. He dropped the laundry basket and grabbed Jackie's wrist. The water was rising faster now, and a loud noise roared from upriver. It sounded like an army of snowplows charging at them.

"Get back to the barn," Al yelled as a wall of water pushed into the side of the house and into the kitchen window.

Robert and Randall hugged a few cans against their chest as they made it to Jackie's side.

"The dam must've failed," one of them said.

The men said more things, but Jackie tuned them out as she watched the river flow into the window where Chubs had just been.

And then he was back in the doorway, holding his grandmother's mirror.

"You idiot," Jackie yelled, one hand waving in the downpour, the other resting on her midsection. "We need you!"

The water wracked the house from every side.

Once, when they were young, not yet engaged, they were cruising the state roads outside the Detroit city limits. Chubs had pulled onto the shoulder of a busy stretch; he told Jackie he'd seen something on the other shoulder and that he'd be right back. She told him not to go; the four lanes were thick with rush hour exhaust. He smiled at her and like that, was in the street, dodging semis and Chevys and Buicks. One end to the other then back again while Jackie leaned against the driver's-side door, the radio singing in the background. He plopped back into the driver seat and handed her something. It was a flower, Queen Anne's lace, a weed, really. A stupid stunt but a bouquet of a gesture.

Chubs tried hiking the mirror up onto his shoulder but couldn't seem to get a firm grip. The house shuddered. Jackie called to him, wanting to wring his neck for grabbing the most impractical thing, wanting him to simply make it back, wanting some idea to come to her that would help her help him do just that. Hating herself for not having told him she was pregnant.

He stepped out onto the porch at the exact wrong moment, when the wind kicked the water up, the clapping hands grabbing at the siding and ripping the porch from the house. Chubs fell backward into the doorway, dropping the mirror into the river. He rose to his knees, braced against the jamb, arms under the water swishing around, feeling for the mirror that was probably already twenty feet downriver. Another wave crashed into him, almost sending him away. The expanse between the barn and the house was now more river than land. Finally, Chubs met Jackie's eyes. If there had been more time, maybe Jackie would have understood Chubs's need to take a chance like this. Maybe, too, he would have realized why she had stopped drinking. Why she had spent so much time working on the second bedroom. Why she had told him eggshell white was a good first coat, no telling who might want to paint it something else.

"Chubs," she cried. "I'm pregnant." She didn't know if she had said it loud enough or if the truth had been lost to the wind and rain.

In a horribly perfect motion, the water lifted the house off its supports and spun it in the current. Jackie stepped forward, losing one of her shoes to the river. She couldn't see Chubs until the house spun around. He was bracing himself in the doorway, but there wasn't anything to him. No tears. No fear. Nothing left for her to salvage for the years to come during those nights when she wouldn't be able to sleep, for the mornings when she looked at herself in the bathroom mirror and saw that doorway and Chubs's deadly acceptance staring back at her.

She threw herself forward toward the image of her husband. The river lapped up her ankles, up her calves, up her waist until she became half river, half woman.

"Jackie," Al shouted. "Jackie, come back!"

She continued after the house. The wind stirred up whitecaps on the surface of the river and branches crashed into the waves. The twins huddled behind Al and spoke in mangled meaningless words as the house spun into the main flow of the river, leveling trees as it went.

"Human chain," Al called. "Now."

Robert and Randall held hands, Robert holding onto the tailgate of his truck as Randall inched out into the water. Al shimmied down the short human rope and circled one arm around Jackie's waist.

"Got you," he said. He pulled her close to him, tucked under his chin. The house hit a wall of jammed logs and curled over it like a horse going over a fence. Jackie couldn't look away. The sound of it, Jesus Christ, the sound of her home as it splintered on the other side of the logs, like chicken bones in a garbage disposal.

The men pulled themselves back to the barn, onto some idea of dry land. Al held Jackie.

"He's gone," she said. "He's gone."

───

There was nothing left the next morning. The men tried to get Jackie to eat but she just lay on a bed of old, forgotten news.

Jackie didn't know about this county, its history. She didn't know anything about FEMA-designated flood plains. She didn't know that she had lost her husband to the worst natural disaster to break the Thumb since the forest fires a century earlier.

She didn't know these new men who stood watching the soup-brown foam bubbles at the edge of the Cass and the whirlpool that spun in the hollow of her home's foundation. They saw her, she knew, as a stranger—homeless, friendless, hopeless, too, even as they issued words of hollow comfort. She didn't know these men. And they would never really know her at all.

———

One week after the rain began, it stopped. Al had hoisted Jackie off the dirt floor and promised her a room in his house for as long as she needed. Until she could recover. Until she could start a new life.

"At least you're alive," he told her as they pulled into his driveway.

As if that even began to explain what she was supposed to do next.

BRIDGE WORK

Bucky's Bridge spans the Cass River on a wooded and mosqui-toed stretch of Outer Road where I've got a place with my wife, Marcy. I always told her that up under that bridge would be the perfect spot for mischief. I was young once and did more than my fair share of jacking things up. I told the police what could go on under that bridge wouldn't be no hoochy-coochying, but does anybody wanna listen to Levon Cutler? You're sure as shit they don't. So, not too long after the police denied my request for more frequent patrols, I took it upon myself to head out to the bridge every night. Just to look around. Keep an eye on things. Marcy thinks it's because I like to keep moving. "Moseying," she calls it. I can hear her joke on the phone when one of the girls calls. I like to think I'm doing what needs to be done. Either way, she likes it and I like that she likes it. It's not the biggest bridge in Michigan or in Tuscola County for that matter, but when you're standing on it looking over the edge, seeing nothing but a canyon of trees and the river so far down, it's like you're flying. It's always like that, except during the flood, but that was fifteen years ago and a fluke. Good thing Marcy and me got a place on the high side of the riverbank.

Most nights are the same. I throw on a jacket, kiss Marcy, grab the flashlight Uncle Sam sent me home with, and when I'm out the door, I tuck my jeans into my socks. Poison oak throughout the summer, you know. I go out when the night starts getting blue from the stars, when the whistle of river frogs mixes with the mosquitoes droning around my head. I keep my light low and red for two reasons: one, so's I don't alert whoever might be under the bridge; two, well, shit, I like how pretty the river is at night. It's damn near magical. One night, though, I get to the bridge, and at the end of a twenty-yard streak of red, I see it.

Funny how blood looks under a red light, like molasses spilled on the kitchen floor. I moved closer to a brown mass slumped against the concrete barrier. *Them cops didn't ever listen*, I thought. I held the light steady and I swear to God I haven't walked so painlessly since '67. My first thought was it was a person. Some somebodies had gotten too carried away in whatever they were up to under Bucky's, and one of them had wound up dead.

"Hey, you all right?" I asked. I was choking on my heartbeat as I crept toward the heap. Gravel crunched behind me, and I flipped the high beam on as I pivoted on my heels, flooding the span of the bridge in white light.

"Who's there," I said. I strained my eyes as if someone or something would just appear on that empty bone of a road. It was nothing but my nerves. A dog barked somewhere as I turned back to the heap and my light reflected off a large sparkling eye.

It was a whitetail deer. I walked up on it hoping that it was fully dead and that it had been quick. I'm a hunter myself, and I can't stomach see-ing the things suffer. I got up to the slumped brown shadow and that's when the smell hit me. Musk, river mud, burst guts. My throat began aching up from my gut and I froze. There ain't no breeze here in August, so I'm anchored on this bridge with the smell, the sound of river frogs screwing, and the lingering thoughts of something horrible going on just below me. Like a murder or one a them satanic love-ins trying to summon up ghosts. My stomach loosened and, mostly, I felt relieved it wasn't a person. But a man still hates being proved wrong.

———

Now, the problem with roadkill around here is the road commission won't clean it up. Something about saving the budget for salt in the winter. But with the smell of that deer and the heat we were having that year, whew, forget about it. So, I set to hauling it up against the barrier so I could toss it over into the river. I wasn't gonna kill myself dragging the thing all the way up the road. I ain't stupid and I ain't young. I hunkered down and pulled its legs up close to the body. Using the concrete barrier, I inched that damned deer up, its head prodding my chest and its face looking up at me. Its gray, dead tongue licking with every heave, I tried my best to keep the body belly up, to keep the guts inside him, to keep him whole, but damned if that thing didn't weigh as much as me. He rolled a bit, and I felt his innards soak my coat. *Jesus*, I thought, and I knew Marcy was gonna kill me when I came home streaked in red and green. I gave up, panting, and let the thing slump back to the road.

I passed my light back along the bridge and noticed a car parked at the far end. Walking up to it, I felt my leg start aching like it does when I work it too much. Had I known a person could get burned so bad their joints don't work right ever again, no matter how good the grafts, I woulda hoofed it down to the Blue Water Bridge and crossed to Canada, free and clear. Maybe Bucky had the right idea if not totally the right—well, I guess execution is the kinda right word. Anyway, I come up on this sharp sedan, new and crisp except for the front driver's side. A crunch of metal and plastic caked in fur and half-digested corn. There was no one inside, so I called out again thinking the driver was probably taking a piss in the woods. Nothing. I walked around the car, shining in the windows. A crack veined across the windshield. Hamburger wrappers and beer cans littered the floorboards. Drinking and driving on a Tuesday night—some people live a charmed life.

"You can't leave this car here," I called. I heard a rumble of stone and a splash from under the bridge. A coughing fit answered me. I made my way around the end of the bridge following the sound like a coyote to a sick rabbit. The mosquitoes fell in love with me. Trying to toss that deer had been a mistake. The aching in my leg became a burning, and I was already too hot. Takes a mighty man to admit he's weak.

I made it through the brush and came out on a slab of granite caked in mud and bird shit. Candy wrappers and broken glass filled the cracks in the stone. Someone had set fire to a tire somewhere along the river, and the remains had washed up under Bucky's. It was like a catchall for the remains of good times, a garbage dump of memories. I could barely make out the river; the trees just suck up the moonlight the farther down the riverbank you go. I flashed down the piles of granite and fell upon someone hunched up on a flood boulder. A kid.

"What you doing down here, boy?"

He looked up and his eyes reflected back at me like the deer's, only blue and colder. Snot ran to his lips, and he had puke down the front of himself. He was a real mess, this kid, a right sight against the white rock, like a popped pimple left to ooze. A semi ran lonely way out on the highway. I thought about my wife and how she'd be lying in bed thinking that I was wasting another night.

"I ain't asking again, son."

"Don't tell my dad," he said.

"Who's your dad?"

"Harold Butcher," he said.

"Don't know him," I said, "can't tell him." The kid just stared at me and started coughing again. A real dry fit, specks of McDonald's flying from his lips. Jesus, I tell you this kid really had himself wound up, like a rubber band ready to be shot. He stared down at the crawling river. *Aw shit*, I thought. My shoulders slouched and whatever I had been feeling above the bridge was washing away underneath it. I walked over and slipped on the red film so's not to blind him. Standing over him, I didn't have any words. No fooling, I raised three girls and didn't have practice with this sort of thing. I just stood there, covered in deer gunk, staring at this kid covered in himself.

"You been drinking, son," I said.

"Please, man, don't tell my dad."

"I told you I ain't telling nobody. What brought you here?"

"I wasn't aiming for here," he said. "If that dumb deer hadn't nailed me, I'd be halfway down to the city by now." He stopped coughing long enough to wipe the snot from his nose.

"What's in the city?"

"What's with the interrogation?"

"Boy, you're hard up in my neck of the woods. Look at this shit." I waved light across the garbage and graffiti. "You're either out here as part of it or you need help. I'm trying to figure out which. Whose car is that?" I stared at him hard. He averted his eyes. I can summon the fear of God when I want to. "Wait, don't say it. If your daddy is any kind of man, he's gonna wring you dry when you get home. I know that's what I'd be doing." I never even spanked my girls, but a lie is a handy tool you keep in the bottom of your toolkit just in case, like a star head screwdriver. Not good for most things but sure as shit handy when you need it.

"He already did that," the kid said. He turned the other side of his face toward the light and goddamn did he have a shiner. It looked like someone had chucked a water balloon filled with blue and green food coloring at the side of his head. "Can I just stay here for a bit and figure out what to do next?"

There was no way to say no to the kid. Jesus, how could I? I set the light down on an overhang of rock and sat down on the granite next to him. He smelled as bad as the deer, as bad as me. A pool of vomit slid down the rock face and out of the circle of light. A muskrat slipped into the river and away from us. We watched the ribbons of moonlit water stream from where the thing cut through the current. I couldn't see past the red light, but I knew: the animal swam effortlessly, as if it were part of the river itself, able to come and go, run or hide as it saw fit.

"Why are you out here, man?" he asked.

"That's what I asked you, boy," I said. He sure was pale but had some muscle to him. I guess he needed to if that bruise on his face was any indication. He must'a been close to eighteen, an unfair, impossible age.

"My dad just bought that car last month," he went on, "barely has a thousand miles on it." He wasn't drunk anymore, not with all of it washing into the river at our feet.

"I live around," I said. "Nasty shit happens out here. You can't trust the cops to do their job right. I keep an eye out."

"Tough guy," he said.

"Name's Levon," I answered. "Or Mr. Cutler." He looked at me from the corner of his eyes and snorted. He was kinda right, I was acting the tough guy. I guess he'd had his fill of that. "What's yours?"

"My name's Scott Butcher," he said.

"Pleasure," I said. I stuck my hand out and he twitched away from it at first. Then he took it and shook, staring down at the motion as if it were the first time he'd seen something like it.

A truck engine's roar came echoing from up the road. This one was booking it. No doubt it was more kids out hot-rodding. It had become a growing pain in the butt in the years since Outer Road got paved. I told the county this was exactly what was gonna happen, but nobody listens to me. Told them that one day someone was gonna hit the curve onto Bucky's Bridge at exactly the wrong speed and they're gonna fly out over the river and drop.

Boom. That'll be the end of 'em, for sure.

The truck rumbled onto the bridge then screeched to a stop, its radio shaking my ears. My stomach knotted and the kid stared a hole up through the bottom of the bridge. Time slowed as we listened for someone to get out. I heard a crash of glass and someone holler. The tires burned and whoever it was was gone. The kid buried his head in his knees. We sat awhile in the red and blue, stinking to beat hell.

"You know why they call it Bucky's Bridge?" I asked.

"Everybody does," he said. "Some guy named Bucky jumped off it forever ago. I heard it was because he was gay and couldn't deal."

I frowned. Some of that was true, but it's stupefying how a moment in time changes the older it gets. Becomes something more than just the facts, and the event of telling the story becomes larger than the event itself.

"Bucky and I grew up together," I said. "He'd've been an old man like me had this place not killed him. I didn't hear about what happened until I came home from the war." I took a moment. I was just trying to give that boy something to listen to. Crashing your daddy's new car isn't much when you think about people dying. And this kid wasn't dead, yet. "He just wanted to get away, I suppose."

"Sounds about right," Scott said. "Ain't anything here." He picked up a handful of gravel and began throwing the stones one by one into the water, each falling with a hollow *plunk*.

The heat that summer had kept Marcy and me inside during the days. She didn't put in a garden that year, saying it was so hot that either she or the plants woulda dropped dead. So, she stayed inside doing crosswords and when the sun got low, we'd putz through our woods and do some birdwatching. The AC was murder on my throat but no way I'd let her drop dead from heat stroke. Anyway, there I sat in all the day's heat that

Bucky's Bridge held up underneath it, along with the trash and the graffiti and the mosquitoes.

Bucky had been one a them boys that preferred to run with the older kids. He couldn't buy the beer—didn't like it, he said, drank Vernor's ginger ale, so much that he always smelled like sugar and ginger—but me and my friends let him hang. Some of the guys felt good having a disposable little brother around. I felt that way about him for a while, too. He was quick to please, like he was auditioning for a permanent spot in the gang. Plus, he always had a few extra bucks on him to chip in. He was a right helpful kid.

Marcy had me on a string before I went to Vietnam, before she became the wifemate. She'd break date plans early in the week just to call me a day later to ask if I had any plans. As if going out was her idea. She said she was *just making sure* I really wanted to run with her. I did. That's why I made the plans in the first place. I wasn't man enough to know that when this woman was *just making sure*, what she was saying was, *want me more*.

I was about to cut myself loose from what I saw was a time-wasting game, but there's Bucky, and he asks, *Love her?* I said I think I did. He bops me right on the forehead and says, *Tell her then.* It hit me that I'd never thought of that before. Well, I said it and here we are fifty years later. Bucky was a good guy like that. He was smart in the short-on-words kind of way. I loved him for that but never got to tell him or thank him.

"You got a sweetheart?" I asked the kid. "Here's not always a place that makes you wanna stay. Sometimes all it takes is a special someone."

Scott grunted and shifted half out of the circle of light.

"Ain't none of the girls here do anything for me," he said.

"Then you got choices," I said. "Change your address or change you attitude."

"Sounds like a fortune cookie," the kid said.

That made me chuckle. It was a Marcy-ism, something she'd say to the girls whenever they were in trouble. Either get right or get gone.

I mopped the sweat running down my neck. The kid started coughing again and I slapped him on the back, you know, get whatever was in him out. Not too hard but enough to set him straight, or straighter than he was.

He had a peace about him after that, like one a man gets when he knows he's got some answering to do.

"C'mon," I said, "the least you can do is help an old man clean up after you." He looked back out toward the river, toward the cement legs that moored the bridge and, I swear, for a second, the air smelled sweet, like Vernor's. He gave me a thumbs up and we clamored past the remnants of questionable goings-on, through the thick brush, and back out to the road. Busted beer bottles speckled the windshield of the boy's car and suds streaked down the hood. He walked right past it without so much as a wink, like he knew it wasn't nothin' compared to the car's front end. We batted flies away from the dead deer.

"Just need a little more *umph* to get him over," I said.

"I got him pretty good," he said.

"Yep, you busted him up." I got down again. "Grab his back end. Don't let him spill out."

He rolled up his sleeves as if he wasn't already filthy. I picked up my end and tucked the snout under my chin and crossed the front legs over his chest, like I was placing him in a casket. The kid got the rear up no sweat. There was going to come a time soon when his daddy wasn't gonna cuff him no more and it'd be a lesson learned the hard way. The deer bled a little on the concrete, blending in with the graffiti, and as we got him up to the top, I felt his insides shift and pull away from us, like whatever was left inside him wanted to jump. It was almost like he flew from our hands. Watching him fall through the blue and disappear, hearing the *thwack* of him hitting the water, I thought of Bucky.

"Shit," Scott said, "the thing bled on me." He held his hands away from himself like they were radioactive.

"What did you expect? You hit it hard enough."

I got the kid back into his daddy's car. He grabbed a handful of the burger wrappers from the floor and tried mopping his hands up.

"Home, then?" I asked. I helped him get the door, too.

He crooked his lips to the side and nodded to me as he started the car. Bits of glass spilled onto the road, and I heard something drag from the undercarriage as he pulled away. There was no way that thing was gonna make it the two hours downstate and he knew it. I watched as the red eyes of his taillights fell behind a rise in the road. The wind kicked up as I turned home. I looked out from the bridge and wondered if the blue was what Bucky saw from the edge. If the river frogs screeched as he flew down to the water. I pictured him diving into the Cass River, turning into a muskrat as his body went under, free.

Enough to Lose

This wasn't long after Alice told me she was ready to start a family. She said we were ready this time, but I think her definition of that word and mine don't exactly match. I was riding shotgun in a no-bells, no-whistles F-150 that was more repairs and patches than actual truck. Rid drove, licking at the chew inside of his bottom lip as he barreled the Ford through the morning, the trailer swaying on the ball hitch. Fifteen minutes from the third house on the list. Half past seven and the humidity already bubbled up from the fields and the smell of dead grass and asphalt baked in the cab. The radio still worked, but the first time I turned it on, Rid had punched it off before half a note sang out. *Don't got time for that*, he'd said. I hadn't touched anything on the dash since, not that any of the rest of the knobs worked anymore. When the July heat caught up with the humidity June had left behind, I found out the crank for my window was busted too. I texted this to the big boss, who ran the operation remotely from a Detroit area code, but all he replied with was the transmission was new, the tires spun, and that was all I needed to get the jobs done.

It was my first day with Secured Properties, mowing lawns for bank repossessions at ten bucks a pop, and I had already inhaled more grass clippings, caked my eyes in more dust, and ridden more backroads than I had known were in Tuscola, Huron, and Genesee Counties. My ma was the one who told me about the job. I hadn't mowed a lawn since my dad had let me lug his push mower around my neighborhood, ringing door-bells and offering my services, and even then, at fourteen, I was raking in at least twenty bucks per. Plus, I could rely on one of the old folks to come out with lemonade or sun tea. I didn't want to take this job, but Pioneer Sugar hadn't returned my calls, not even for a seasonal position, and there was no way I was going to corral carts for Walmart ever again. Alice sold Wrap-It—a plastic body wrap that was supposed to help people lose weight—from our home and at parties she organized. She had only been able to get her sister and my ma to work for her full time, so the money only trickled in. I didn't want the job, but I needed it. So, I called Secured, passed a piss test, signed a W-9, and drove out to the company garage when the new pay cycle started. That's where I met Ridley Bellows Jr., leaning against the loaded trailer, sipping a gas station coffee.

"Morning," I'd said. "Name's Tim Darling." I'd held out my hand. "You must be Ridley. The boss said you get out here early."

"Gives me more time for more jobs," he'd told me. He shook my hand, not so much limp, as if he were a weak man, but as if he didn't want to bother. Like he didn't have anything to prove to me. "Got everything loaded this time but tomorrow you gotta get here early to help out. Let's go." We'd climbed in and pulled onto the dirt road, heading straight to our first yard.

The year 2008 was bad for most people. Normal people. Bank people. People caught somewhere in between felt it harder and for longer than most. I was one of the in-between people. Alice and I got by, lost some things along the way—evicted when our landlord let our first apartment go into default—but still had enough to feel more or less human. We married out of high school and were already coming up on ten years hitched. For the last two years, her cousin rented a duplex to us on a road that butted up to the Cass River. I had a few semesters' worth of college in me, but the only thing I'd learned was that I could spend more than my share of time and money on something and still not feel like I'd learned anything at all. But I promised Alice, and she me, that we'd get enough put away and get ourselves a place.

The banks that came out of '08 ahead had more properties than they knew what to do with. That's where the in-betweeners like me and Rid came in. We kept those properties looking livable until they sold. Nobody wants to buy a shack sinking into a yard of chin-high weeds, and if a house looked like someone lived there, so the logic went, they wouldn't become the target of vandalism. We'd pull up to a double-wide or a split-level out in the country, and before we unloaded, Rid walked around the whole place with a cheap digital camera, snapping shots of the house and yard. These were the before shots. Then, once we finished with the job, he'd go back and snap the after shots.

"So we can prove we did the job and didn't screw it up or break in or anything," he said.

Rid didn't say much that wasn't related to the job. At the first property of the day, he circled the house with a Weedwacker while I wrangled with the mower. I'd never been on a zero-turn mower before, one of those speedy numbers that wasn't much more than a rubber seat cushion bolted above three sets of blades and a set of levers used for acceleration and steering. Just a nudge would gun that sucker along, and if you didn't give both those big levers the same amount of love, the whole thing would start spinning out of control like some redneck hovercraft.

"Lines gotta be straighter," Rid said. "Lines gotta be straighter." I swerved down the lawn, taking a wide turn at the road and made my way back toward the house. "For the grace and love of naked baby Jesus, kid, you speak English? The big boss don't pay if the job looks like shit. Straighten those lines out!" The wind kicked clippings into my eyes and I jerked the mower side to side as I looped around the lawn. The job looked like hell, even after Rid tried a quick touch-up, and he still had to blur the after photos just enough to hide what looked like a drunk haircut. That first house, a boarded-up cottage on a half acre, took forty-five minutes. In the truck, pushing past sixty, Rid let me have it.

"Fifteen minutes per job, max. Got it?" he said. "Thirty-minute drive time between jobs. That paces out to twenty bucks an hour. You just cut that in half."

"Sorry, Ridley," I said. "It's my first time out."

"A job worth doing is worth doing right and quickly. The *first* time. Hear me?" he said. He was all cheekbones and nose and his eyes got real narrow, as if he were daring me to not answer.

"First time," I said. "Gotcha."

"And call me Rid, only my ma called me Ridley." By noon, he had rolled the sleeves of his T-shirt over his shoulders and I could see his veins. He looked like a burlap bag pulled tight over a classroom skeleton.

And that was Rid. Twenty bucks an hour, speeding from one vacant house to the next with a twenty-seven-year-old nobody in tow and a work list that looped and spiraled wider and wider as more jobs came in. We started that first week mowing the abandoned summer houses in Caseville, and by the weekend, we'd wound up halfway to Flint spraying weed killer outside foreclosed apartment complexes.

When the next pay cycle started, we were back up along Saginaw Bay, mowing those same summer houses. They stopped being homes by the time Rid and I got to them; they were only a crisp ten-dollar bill, calluses, and heat rash to us. It only took a couple more screwups on the zero-turn and an earful from Rid before it all became routine to me. Pull in, unload, before shots, mow, weed, trim, after shots, load out, move on. Seventeen or so hours a day. As long as I could keep up with Rid's pace, the paychecks would be heavy.

———

A month in, I parked outside the duplex, beyond beat. I stayed out, listening to the grind of cicadas through the open windows of my truck, drinking a tall boy. The lights inside were off. Alice went to bed early so she could get to the gym at five to sell to the before-work crowd. The owner let her sell from a booth she set up behind the StairMasters, and she pushed a sale or two most days. She passed her afternoons at home, posting to Facebook and fitness boards, trying to sign up enough people to earn a promotion from her higher-ups. Her sister managed to sign up some of her friends for a while. Those were a few good months. Alice had enough wraps and diet pills going out that we paid off one of the Mastercards. Then the school year kicked in and her sister's friends went back to class and stopped selling. Things got tight again, and we maxed out the Visa. That's how things go. I was used to the up and down just so long as I could punch a clock and get another day behind me. Why bother looking back when you're never going to get closer to those days? That's just how time works, a straight line. But I confess, in those few moments alone in the dark car, maybe a little drunk, looking at the stained vinyl siding of my life, I'd pull the photo I kept behind the sun visor and think about the boy. The son Alice and I gave up when we were seventeen. I didn't have to look at the picture much by then, I already knew, no matter how long I stared at it, that I couldn't see him growing inside Alice. It was a wrinkled four-by-six snapshot that happened to find Alice and me standing next to each other outside our high school cafeteria. I had my arm around her waist and was trying to kiss her, plant a sloppy one on her that only teenagers have the balls to get away with. But the wrinkled moment isn't the kiss, it's the half second where she pulled away and I missed. To anyone else it'd look like I was leaning to kiss her belly, our boy. But I know better.

He came a day after we turned our graduation tassels. Ten round pounds, twenty-one inches. A big, heathy boy with ten fingers and toes and adoptive parents sitting out in the lobby waiting to meet him. Waiting to take him from us. All the papers signed and nothing left but the "thanks a lots" and the "have a nice lifes." When the nurse wrapped him and handed him to Alice, he didn't curl up to her. It was as if he knew, like he had heard from inside Alice when we interviewed couples who wanted him and could care for him. Maybe he felt it when Alice reached out to shake the hands of the couple we finally found, and when their hands met, all the love and connection a boy can have for his mother pulsed from Alice's belly, down her arm, and into the bodies of his new mom and dad. When Alice brushed his cheek with her finger, he turned away and stared past her arms, past me, to the door of the delivery room. I can't forget his dark brown eyes. He had my father's eyes.

I finished my beer and took the empties inside, lining them on the kitchen counter with the other returnables, about three dollars' worth. There was a note on the fridge: *T., No sales today. Return bottles tomorrow. Buy bread. Love, A.* The mugginess in the living room escaped from a cracked window, and in the quiet, the breeze sounded like music. I didn't want to wake Alice with my smell. Sweat and two-stroke gasoline doesn't make for good company in bed. I left my grass-stained clothes in a pile at the end of the couch and sat down in my underwear. If Alice had come out to see me, I wonder if she'd have said that I was what ready looked like.

It was noon a few weeks later when the big boss texted me a new job: a ranch in a cul-de-sac outside Caro. We were supposed to get an updated list of jobs at the beginning of each pay period, but if a quicky like this came across the wire, the boss would forward it to us. He never passed on one. The banks paid Secured Properties forty bucks per job, so for every ten Rid and I made, the boss made twenty. We were also only one of three teams the boss had running across the region, so I can only imagine how nice it was to be him. At least he paid for the gas and never bounced a paycheck.

"Got a quicky," I said, "near Caro."

"Christ," Rid said, "that's twenty minutes the other way." By that time, Rid and I had found our way to communicate with each other, born from spending too much time together doing the same thing until it became instinct. Rid wasn't the kind of guy to double back. Our second week together, the Weedwacker kicked up a face full of poison ivy and he couldn't see straight for a few days. He had me drive, and it only took me missing a couple turns—no more than a few minutes burned—before he booted me back over to shotgun. Twenty minutes was a lifetime to Rid. Either that or it was the line that separated life moving forward and life standing still.

"C'mon, Rid. It's ten bucks now instead of next payday. I know it's worth my time."

"You're the kind of guy who stops to pick up a dime, aren't you?" He rolled his fingers along the steering wheel.

"And you're not?" The job we were coming from had a small stable and corral overgrown with Queen Anne's lace and dandelions that hid piles of sunbaked horse shit. The first hit with the zero-turn sent a cloud of it raining onto the two of us. By the time we'd loaded up from there, we smelled like the type of guys who would stop to pick up a penny.

"Only if it's right in front of me," Rid said. He kept the truck straight. "Plus it looks like it's gonna storm soon. Got two jobs right next to each other coming up soon."

"Yeah, but we're driving into the storm. It could start any minute. Better ten bucks now than *maybe* twenty later." The truck moved on. "Rid, the boss wants it done. I need the sure cash. We're going. We can get back to Caro in fifteen minutes the way you drive."

"Shit, kid. What's with you?"

"Need the cash."

"We all need the cash," he said.

"The wife and I want a house. Want it sooner than later."

"Takes a lot of lawn mowing to buy a house."

"She used to babysit her cousins but they're old enough to be on their own now. She's been selling Wrap-It for about a year now."

"What's that?"

"You know, it's a body wrap type deal. You stretch it around your waist and thighs and it makes you thinner."

"So, she sells girdles?"

"These make you lose weight. Like the ones on those late-night infomercials. Only Alice sells them in person. Hired a few people to sell for her."

"Like Tupperware and dildos?"

"What? Jesus, no," I said. "They're weight-loss apparel."

"How do you lose weight with them?" he asked.

"I don't know but my wife says it works. She sells diet pills, too." He looked at me as if I had just thrown up in my lap. I remembered the first time Alice came home with a neon blue brochure filled with men and women with huge smiles, wearing nothing but underwear and their wraps. She said someone had an info desk set up at the laundromat and had told her all about the benefits and earning potential while our linens were on the spin cycle. I love Alice, always have, and it's that love that kept me calm when the first shipment of wraps came and I opened a box of what looked more like flesh-colored cling wrap and caffeine pills than a good investment. She was thrilled, though, and kept saying that this wasn't just a second income, it was her ticket to getting back into the body she had "before." It never bothered me that I didn't know anybody who was in the same shape as they were when they were seventeen because I think Alice knew that to be in a seventeen-year-old body when you're pushing twenty-seven wasn't just unrealistic, it was unhealthy. What bothered me was the way she always said it: *before*. Period. As if the boy was an edit cut off the end of her sentences, off her memories from when we were kids.

"We do what we can," I said. The road hummed under the truck as Rid pushed toward the dark clouds in the west.

"Alright, kid," he pulled onto the shoulder of the highway, "we'll head back to Caro. Looks like we ain't beating the rain."

Rid turned down the cul-de-sac and kept the truck slow as we passed a line of houses with actual people living in them. Two-car families one right after the other with wives and husbands and children. Lawns that people mowed themselves. Or lawns that people paid teenagers to mow. People who had made it. The job came up on the right just before the loop, a lawn so overgrown that it folded back onto itself in matted, brown clumps. Weeds cluttered along the sides of the house and the edges of the driveway. The top of a Realtor sign poked through the mess like the face of a friend in a crowd of strangers. Price Reduced in red letters.

"Shit," Rid said. "Looks like nobody's had this job on their list. It's gonna take us over an hour to mow this place, not to mention the time to rake all that shit up." He glared at me and I saw him calculating all the money he wasn't making now that we had committed to this one job. He parked the truck in the street and we climbed out. From the house, I heard someone yell to us. In the shadow on the porch, propped back in a plastic lawn chair, a man in faded jeans and a torn flannel looked out to Rid and me.

"You people are late," the man said. He ran a hand down the stubble on his cheek.

"Excuse me?" I said. "This job just came to us."

"I don't pay you to *not* mow my lawn." Rid and I looked at each other and we both shrugged.

"You don't pay us, man," Rid said. "The banks do. They own this place."

"That's only 'til the loan papers go through." The man rocked in his lawn chair and began to laugh. "Been taking a little longer than I'd planned but don't you worry, loan's coming, and I'll be moved back in quicker than it's taken you to mow this place." He didn't get up to talk to us, he was happy to just sit in his chair and yell across the yard. I looked around the neighborhood. I could hear the screams of children playing in one of the backyards, and someone had fired up their grill with too much lighter fluid.

"Alright," Rid said. He turned to me, "C'mon, let's get this job done. We're gonna get rained on. I'd rather be less wet than more when we finish." He pulled on his leather gloves and dug into the bed of the truck while I lowered the trailer's tailgate.

I mowed along the side of the house slower than what Rid would've liked but I wanted to get a look at the man. A bed roll was laid along the back of the porch and empty tin cans stood lined against the house. When Rid passed the front of the porch with the Weedwacker, I saw the man point and mouth something to him. I couldn't hear over the mower, but it looked like Rid was trying hard to ignore him and just get the job done.

Halfway done with the backyard and the rain came. Quicker than I had thought and harder than I had wanted. Damp grass didn't stop Rid and me, but this was too much. I killed the zero-turn and ran to the truck just as Rid was chucking a pair of clippers into the bed.

"Goddammit," he said. He slammed his door, wiping water from his face. "You know we're not getting paid for this. And the day's shot, can't mow soaked grass and make it look good for the pictures." I wiped my face on my sleeve and leaned back. Fat drops pounded the truck, and I wished I were back at home on the couch listening to the wind and Alice snoring in the bedroom.

"Well, we started early today," I said.

"We only got eight jobs in, so starting early don't mean much, does it?"

"Better than nothing," I said. I looked out toward the house and the man. He was standing now at the edge of the porch, positioning the empty tin cans under cracks in the eaves trough to catch the rain.

"This isn't much more than nothing," Rid said. He had his hand over his eyes as if the rain had been more an inconvenience to him than anybody else. Like it was an insult. "Get me my lipsmoke out of the glove box," he said.

"Your what?"

"Chew, kid. Got a tin in there. Get it." I popped open the glove box and sitting on top of the truck's manual was a handful of tins all with their labels ripped off. I grabbed one on top. "Not that one," Rid said. "Can't you read?"

"Read what?" I looked down at the tin in my hands and saw a length of Scotch tape stuck across the top that said *Thursday*. The ink of the letters filled the tiny grooves of the tape, making the writing look old, like the tin had seen so many Thursdays that it knew nothing else.

"Move," Rid said. He leaned across the bench and grabbed another tin.

He popped it open and wedged a healthy pinch under his lip. "We'll wait to see if this passes. If not, we'll load out." He tucked the tin under his thigh and looked up to the house. "Been doing this job for years now. Mowed a thousand lawns three times over and you know how many times I've run into shit like this?"

"A few?" I asked.

"Zero. Zilch. Goose egg. And do you know why?"

"No."

"Because most people know there aren't any do-overs." He cracked his door, spit, and came back dragging his teeth up his bottom lip. "People like our friend out there don't get that." He leaned back in his seat and closed his eyes.

I watched the rain for another half hour without many more words. A couple times, Rid cracked his door to spit. The man on the porch tended to his tins of rainwater. He didn't pay us any mind once the rain fell. It looked like even in his situation, he still had the ability to separate the necessary from the secondary. A mowed lawn means nothing to a thirsty man.

———

I was home early that afternoon, soaked.

"Mowing at the bottom of a lake?" Alice asked. She puckered her lips like a fish at me from over her laptop.

"I know, right?" I said.

"Don't think about leaving those clothes in a pile," she said. "Put them in a plastic bag. Tomorrow's laundry day."

I grabbed a balled-up Walmart bag from under the sink and went into the bedroom to change.

"How was today?" I asked.

"Sold a wrap," she called. "Got a lady's email. Said she'd be interested in selling, too." I didn't know much about Wrap-It, but Alice told me that if she could sign up three full-time sellers, her immediate boss would give her a larger percentage of what they sold. She had a hard time keeping her sister on board. Alice had me convince my ma to sign up and I remember the look on her face when I told her about it. It was the same look that Rid gave me.

"Do you think she'll sign up?" I asked. I came out in a pair of gym shorts and a stained Beatles T-shirt.

"She should." She didn't look up from the message board she was posting to. "What's for dinner?"

I opened the fridge and just stared. A few cans of tuna. Eggs. Half-gone gallon of milk. Loaf of bread. Mason jar of pickled asparagus my ma had made. Mustard bottle propped upside down so what was left didn't crust on the bottom. "Tuna sandwiches," I said.

"Wonderful!"

"Babe, it's only tuna," I said.

"What? No, no I've been messaging this woman. She lives in Detroit. Says she is interested in selling." She tapped at the keyboard and didn't look up. "Just think, if I sign her up by the end of the week, I'll have a foothold in a whole new market. More people means more buyers." I turned on the stove and started mixing the tuna and eggs. "Then if she signs up a few more people, that automatically places me in the Sapphire Salesman category."

"And that's a good thing, right?" I dug in the cupboard for some salt and pepper.

"Of course it's a good thing." She turned to me, propped up on the arm of the couch. "That means I can start selling the Pro-Fit style wraps and vitamins!"

"And those are better than what you're selling now?"

"I would guess so." She got up and pulled down her pants. "See?" She had wraps around her butt and her thighs, stretched past the elastic of her panties. With her pants around her ankles, she shimmied around to show me her backside. "This Basic-Fit style just comes in a rectangle shape. The Pro-Fit forms to curves and targets trouble areas."

"And what does that mean?" It looked to me like my wife was wearing a sweaty diaper, so I thought I was allowed to be a little confused. She pulled her pants up and fell back to her laptop.

"It means more money, Timothy."

There was a silence while I mixed the ingredients into a passable meal.

"And who can beat that?" I said.

I scooped up a handful of eggy tuna and molded it into patties before sliding them into the pan. I watched the oil pop and hiss from under them and thought about the man and his cans of water. I could live on canned tuna just fine, and I was sure even the pickiest of eaters would eventually get used to it. But when I'd seen that row of cans, placed just so under the steady streams of gutter runoff, a part of me planted itself into that lawn like a patch of crab grass, unable to move, unable to forget.

Every ten days or so, that ranch rotated to the top of the list, and before we could unload the equipment, the man would holler from his lawn chair.

"You guys should be out here once a week. Grass grows too quickly to have you slacking off." Beyond the snort he gave when we parked outside the house, it was easy for Rid to ignore the guy. He just put his ear protectors on, cranked the edger or the Weedwacker or the clippers on, and went to work.

But it wasn't that easy for me. Every time I swung the mower close to the house, I'd stare at the man. He wasn't old, around forty, forty-five. The age where you have enough to lose that you'll lose yourself in the process of trying to hold onto everything. The third time we hit that place, I put half of a sandwich I'd bought on the front step before I hopped on the mower. I nodded at the man before walking back to the truck, but all he did was suck on his lip and shout to Rid that he'd better make sure to not crack the siding with the edger. The next time we stopped out, I found that bag wedged under the propane tank out back. Looked like a raccoon had gotten to it.

Five months into the job, Alice told me that she'd stopped taking her birth control. I came out of the shower and she was sitting, tapping away at the laptop, scrolling past pictures of people in underwear and cellophane. Her telling me that immediately aged me a couple years. I asked her why and she pointed at the computer screen and read: "Too many toxins, like alcohol, drugs, and even contraceptives, can hinder the effectiveness of Wrap-It products. Besides," she said, "we're ready."

It was past six, the sun had just come up, and Rid and I were pulling out of the day's first job. On the highway, heading toward the ranch outside Caro, I couldn't stop replaying the non-conversation Alice and I had had the night before. Rid had been hollering at me while I was on the mower, but I didn't hear him. To hell with the straight line.

"You go stupid overnight, kid?" He asked. "Or you just not care?"

"Sorry, Rid. I got lost in my head. That's all."

"Lost? This job doesn't need a map." He slowed as we came close to Caro.

"It's my wife," I started. "We got into it last night."

"Fighting with the woman, eh. First time I ever heard of such a thing."

"Well, you see we don't fight. She just kinda, you know, tells. And that's that."

"What? You go out with the buds too much? She find a girly mag on the back of the toilet?"

"She wants to start a family."

Rid looked over to me and just stared. Lines of dust were folded into the creases of his mouth and dry grass stuck to the hair at his temples. "So what's the fucking problem?"

"We don't own a home yet," I said.

"So what?"

"So, how are you supposed to raise a kid without a house?" I knew I was talking at a guy who I had no business talking at. And maybe he was thinking, *Who the hell does this kid think he is?* but I didn't feel the need to justify myself. Sometimes you just want to talk and damn whomever is stuck listening to you. "There's a way of things, Rid," I said. "A plan of action."

"It's all broad strokes, kid," he said.

"Excuse me?"

"You heard me. All this," he waved his hand over the steering wheel, across the windshield. "Chaos." He turned down a dirt road. The way he said it, so convinced, maybe not of what he was saying but in himself saying it, sounded like a man familiar with stupidity. He'd seen a world of zero-turn know-nothings and empty houses. He'd heard too many people say too many things about everything from bank loans to weight-loss Reynolds Wrap. And he didn't buy any of it. He just wanted his jobs, one at a time, looping forever. Part of me hated him at that moment, hated the dismissal of how the world was according to eyes that weren't his, but also knowing that he'd probably been some kind of stupid at some point in his life.

"Yeah, but—"

"But what?" he asked. "But nothing. So your old lady wants you to throw one in her? That's her right and who are you to keep that from her?" He pulled into the cul-de-sac. "Not what you had planned? Tough, man up and do it." He stopped the car before we got to the house. "Now what in Jesus's pecs is this righteous mess?" Out the windshield we saw two police cruisers parked in the yard, cherrytops blazing.

"Might as well pull up and see what's what," I said. A cop met us outside the house.

"What do you two want?"

"We're with Secured Properties," Rid said. "We're the guys who take care of this place."

"Not today, you're not," the cop said. He looked into the back of the truck and then at me.

"What happened?" I asked.

"Neighbors heard a crash and saw someone moving around inside. You happen to know the squatter here?"

"No," I said. Rid shook his head and looked at his watch.

"But you knew he was living on the front porch?"

"Not my job to report the homeless," Rid said. The officer looked over his sunglasses at him and clicked his teeth.

"We only cut the grass, sir," I said. "The guy sat on the porch and watched us, nothing else. Been here every time we've come around." I heard someone yell from the house.

"I told you, I'm waiting on the loan. Call the bank. Call them!" The man came from the front door, handcuffed and pushed by two officers. They led him to the back of one of the cruisers. I watched as they tucked his head past the doorframe and could feel the officer's hand on my own head. Feel the fingers as they matted my hair and locked me away.

"He busted in the front window," the officer said. "We found him asleep on the living room floor, using a landscape brick as a pillow. Listen, you guys aren't working here today."

"We don't work, we don't get paid," Rid said.

The cop didn't listen. He tapped on the hood of the truck and walked toward the cruisers, pointing and directing the other cops. The car with the man backed out of the lawn, tire tracks rutted into the soft earth, and I wondered how Rid would hide them in the after pictures. As the cruiser passed us, I looked for the man. Here was someone who was being kicked out of his house for the second time. The first time for failing to keep it, the second time for succeeding to get back in it. What else was left for him? I didn't know but I thought that maybe, if I could see the man, see his eyes, have them tell me across the space of two passing cars that this was all right, that I'd get my answer. I needed that. But I didn't see the man. He must've laid himself down in the backseat because it was like he disappeared as soon as the car left the property, as if, without the house, the man was nothing.

———

"Here." I handed Alice the picture I'd kept in the truck and walked to the kitchen to start dinner.

"What's this?"

"It's us," I said.

"Where did you get it? Did your mother find it?"

"It's just been around."

She smiled and pulled her laptop from her knees, folding it on the couch next to her. She came next to me at the sink, wrapped an arm around my waist, and held the picture in front of us.

"That was back when people liked you," she said. She squeezed me.

"And when I didn't talk back," I answered.

"You've always talked back," she said. She unwrapped herself from me and set the picture on the sill above the sink. We'd been saying the same thing to each other for forever. My grandfather used to say it to my mother and then to me when I got older. He passed before Alice came around, but she picked up on it anyway.

"You could trade me in for a model that doesn't," I said. She was back on the couch now, laptop opened. I peeled some carrots.

"No," she said, "I think you're worth keeping." She leaned toward her laptop and scrolled through more pictures.

———

Rid and I parked in front of the house the next day. Plywood replaced where the front window had been. Police tape crisscrossed the porch. We got out of the truck and the smell of lighter fluid blew across the neighborhood. I heard the kids scream again, and though I wanted to keep my thoughts of the boy tucked behind my sun visor, my mind focused on him. He'd be just about ten years old. On the ride home the night before, I'd thought real hard about walking into the bedroom and waking Alice up. Tell her no. Tell her that ready isn't a vinyl-sided duplex and plastic wrap. Ready wasn't ready just because you said it was. I wanted to tell her she was wrong.

But I didn't. After dinner, Alice joined me in the shower and we stayed in there until the hot water ran out.

"So," Rid started, "I'll get the weeds, you tackle the yard. Fifteen minutes. Easy as that."

"Sure thing," I answered. I climbed up on the zero-turn and started her up. I wheeled it up and down the front yard, past the porch where the man had watched us all those weeks. His bedroll and cans were gone; his chair tipped over the edge of the porch.

I spun the mower around at the street and let it idle. The yard stretched below me, the straight line of newly mown grass wedged between an expanse of shag, and for a moment, I swore I could see the grass I had just cut begin to grow again.

THE RUN

I moved into a studio apartment right after I turned thirty, right after Ma passed. Even if the house was paid off, it didn't feel right, me just hanging around a place big enough for a family. Back then, I was working for Pioneer Sugar out at their Caro factory. I was only a seasonal guy, earning fourteen bucks an hour handling a piece of shit frontend loader, spending fifty hours a week piling sugar beets, staging them for the slicers and boiling vats. It was enough for rent, gas in my Grand Am, and food in the fridge while I decided whether to hand Ma's keys over to a Realtor. The time and a half I got never made it home though. I figured the extra cash was just that, extra, and I can't be blamed for wanting to treat myself when the time called for it. I spent most of my off time popping into one or two of the bars that dotted the backroads of Tuscola County. They were everywhere, like screws in drywall, and I enjoyed my regular spots.

A few times after high school, I'd gone down to East Lansing to see my ex-girlfriend Amber Cutler at Michigan State. She'd take me down a road with a cluster of bars where we could slip in underage. The give and take of that was the masses of college kids, the crowded, pukey sidewalks, and the feeling that, on foot, the night became a single blurry blob. It was close enough to fun but once she started dating Rachel, she stopped going out. I guess I wouldn't have wanted to third wheel, anyway. Besides, there is something about these isolated towns up here in the Thumb, something about the miles of road stitched between them, where buckshot riddles the speed limit signs and the night sky isn't washed out with streetlights, that's better, safer than any walk down a city block.

One Friday night, I was slumped at a back table way down in Kingston drinking a Bud Light, waiting for Scott Butcher to roll in and watch the game with me. The place was dead, Kingston Tap always was. The weekend crowd never ran that far south, and I liked it that way. There were only five others sitting at the bar. A line of empty tables and fake leather chairs filled the empty space between me and the door. Aside from the Coors mirror behind the bar and a rusty mill saw above the TV, the walls were bare. I think the place only stayed open out of habit, but it was quiet, and Mac behind the bar hadn't changed his prices in forever. It was a good place to catch a game and a ten-dollar buzz. Sometimes Mac cooked hot dogs on a Weber grill he kept out back and sold them for a buck. Sometimes he just gave them away. That night had been one of those giveaway nights, and I had already mowed through three. The Tigers were tied 1–1 on the giant Magnavox that stood along the far wall. Not a bad start to a Friday night, I thought.

A truck skidded into the parking lot. I heard Mötley Crüe through the walls, "Dr. Feelgood," Scott's favorite. A few of the old men turned to the door, some shaking their heads. Scott didn't kill the engine until the song finished, then he slammed the truck door. He hipped the bar door open hard but didn't flinch as he beelined for the bar.

"Hey, Mac, you minor-serving hilljack, get me a beer. And make sure you scrape the foam off the top. I ain't paying for air. Alright? Alright." He laughed and rapped his knuckles on the bar. Though he was a little shorter than me, Scott was a big guy with no extra stretch of skin spared to cover him. He'd started losing hair right out of high school and was now in the habit of shaving himself bald. He looked like a stocky Mr. Clean, but instead of a spotless white wardrobe, he preferred faded black jeans and a rotation of old jerseys. That night he was on brand with a Magglio Ordóñez jersey stained along the hem and collar. He strolled toward me, nodding and offering half smiles to the men, most of whom had already turned away from him and back to their beers.

He pulled up a chair.

"Dick, buddy," he said, "we hitting the Run tonight?"

"The Run?" I asked.

"Yeah, man. Been a while."

Folks called the country roads stitching the countryside together the Run, a night's shot to all the Thumb bars from Caro to Bad Axe and all them places in between: Colwood, Gagetown, even out to Deckerville. Two pitchers at each stop before 2 a.m. When we were younger, Scott and I would hit a couple of these joints on Friday or Saturday nights when the only other thing we'd be doing was a lot of nothing. Sometimes, we'd make it to a third or fourth place if we heard it was smashing with more than just the old, field-hand-and-beer-gut crowd. One time, years before, the O'Connor sisters were home from their college lives. We let them pull us along toward Colwood, the fourth joint of the night. We never made it. Instead, we woke up at the bottom of a tiling ditch with shit-filled runoff from a sugar beet field pooling at the floorboards of Scott's Silverado 2500. That was his third DUI, when the court took his license and what was left of his truck. I kissed his windshield pretty hard when we hit the bottom of that ditch, lost some teeth on the right side, the sharp ones. The county saw that as "serious bodily injury" and locked Scott up for six months. We never saw the O'Connor girls again. No matter. They moved out of the Thumb, and I hear Krissy married an engineer down in Detroit and Denise won the lottery and moved overseas. Just like that.

"We're a little far out to hit the Run," I said. *We're a little old for that*, is what I almost said.

"I ain't talking about here." He leaned back, balancing the chair on its hind legs. "You think any'a them kids wanna waste the gas to come out to this shithole?" I licked mustard off my finger. I don't remember a time that I hadn't known Scott. Growing up, he was at my place more times than not, for dinner or Nintendo, anything to keep him out of his own house and away from his dad. In school, he seemed like the kind of kid who needed a friend, and some part of me at the time felt pride that I was the one who could be that person. He failed the third grade and I started school late, so it just felt right. We used to shoot hoops at recess and flick pea stones at the pretty girls on the playground. Amber never really liked him, but that kinda proved the point.

"Hey, man," Mac called from the bar, "here's your beer. No bottle service *in this shithole*." He shoved the pitcher onto the bar, sloshing beer down its sides. Scott shot up and brought back the goods. He poured himself half a glass, downed it, then filled it before pouring one for me.

"So I can catch up," he said between gulps.

I preferred Bud to Busch Light and he knew it, but getting the guy to shell out an extra buck for it was like pulling teeth. I got a kick out of hounding him for it; I think he only drank Busch to hear me gripe.

He'd gotten a third glass, as always, and set it off to the side of the table within reach. His spitter, so he could scoop it up and cuddle his bottom lip against it and let a goober of Kodiak spit slop down the side until it pooled at the bottom.

"So whaddya think?" he said. I saw his tongue wedging between his teeth and lip as he waited for me to answer.

"I don't know, man." I looked around the bar and wondered if Mac was grilling any more hot dogs. "I should head back to Ma's and pack up more of her stuff." I spent large chunks of those days avoiding packing up what she had left behind. Even with my things moved into the apartment, the house was miles away from market ready. I had a hard time with her clothing, what I thought she'd want donated, and what I maybe could have sold. The attic, though already boxed up, was filled with enough memories and junk that I had decided to put off dealing with it until after my contract ended at Pioneer. Ma collected Snowbabies, and they populated every shelf and cabinet throughout the place. She knew every year I would get her one for Christmas but still found something about the ceramic doll to fawn over. It didn't seem right to get rid of them. Some things shouldn't be boxed up. I had Ma cremated even though we were technically Catholic, on Easter and Christmas mostly, and was lost on where I was going to pour her out.

"Oh, c'mon, man," Scott insisted. "Let's get in on this. Her shit isn't going anywhere between now and tomorrow morning." He finished his beer and poured another. "Besides, you got Saturdays off and you might find someone worth warming up to."

"It's not shit," I said.

"Right," he said, "my bad. Your mom's precious collection of dolls and state spoons will be A-OK, Dick. Besides, you can afford some time away from all that, not like you've got anyone harping at you to get it done." He winked at me. I thought about the people who had filtered through Ma's house at her wake. Retired teachers, former students, distant cousins passing between the kitchen and living room, pointing at the pictures on the wall and whispering "what now" and "poor Richard" just softly enough for me to pretend I couldn't hear.

Amber had come in for Ma's funeral and stayed a day extra to help clean. We'd kept in touch, even after she graduated from Michigan State and moved even farther away, and I believed we were as close as friends in different states could be. *You should sell this place and come out to Chicago*, she'd said. *Rach can probably put you in touch with a construction crew.* She had explained how her neighborhood was "up and coming," but I couldn't really get what that meant or how I would fit in. Amber had become a Realtor and Rachel was an architect or city planner, something like that. The two owned a townhouse with an extra room they'd offered to rent me. From the sounds of it, the whole area was choked with people who had money and were eager to spend it at all the new places being built. My role in all that seemed like it would stop once those places went up and the grand openings had come and gone. The people who build the boutiques aren't the people shopping in them. I wasn't convinced the move was for me, but that didn't stop Amber from blowing up my cellphone with voicemails and texts, urging me to sell, move, and start over.

Scott, on the other hand, hadn't worked in over two years. His last job had been a five-year stint at a family-owned lumberyard in Caro, working under the owner's punk son, a small-town dynasty heel who loved to remind anybody with an ear who his daddy was. He had kept Scott out in the yard as a minimum wage gofer. The job itself seemed to suit Scott just fine, but he didn't care much for Edwin, the boss. The kid was a good five or six years younger than Scott and that didn't sit well with him, to see a kid flashing his silver spoon in the faces of his employees. Scott spent three days a week camped out in one of the sheds, chain-smoking Marlboros, waiting for customers to pull into the yard, and avoiding the office until closing time.

We were both twenty-seven the summer the lumberyard went up in flames. I've never heard of cigarette ash setting lumber on fire, but Edwin and his daddy said the weather-treated stuff could go up as quick as a snap on a hot day. It seemed pretty farfetched to me then, still does, and the city police thought just the same. They chalked it up as an unfortunate accident. Still, they held Scott for two days while they sorted everything out, and when they released him, he had me drive him to the closest Speedway to stock up on chew. I never saw him smoke another cigarette after that. Since then, he'd rotated between working just long enough to qualify for unemployment, all the while trying to qualify for an SSI check. He said the heavy lifting at the lumberyard had wrecked his back and stopped him from keeping another job. He didn't own a phone and used to come over and use Ma's landline to harass Social Security, but when she caught him drunk dialing them one afternoon, she got so heated that I thought she was going to swat his ass right there in the kitchen. That was the end of that.

I looked down at my watch and remembered thinking about when we started hitting up those one-bar towns and how we'd close a place down without so much as a worry for the next day. Then I thought about where I would store Ma's stuff and if I had enough set aside to pay for a storage unit.

I told Scott that I'd make the Run with him, why not? And just like that, he had his dancing partner. We killed the pitcher in record time and before I could change my mind, we'd jumped in his truck.

———

First, we headed north to Owendale in Scott's S-10. He drove. It was starting to get dark, and even though it was only late spring, you could barely see the tree lines past the acres of corn. It had been warm and wet all month and everything, it seemed, was caked with a layer of mud. The sun had sunk so low only the tops of the cell towers caught the last pulse of light. The cornstalks, thick and dark in the evening half-light, walled in the road like a tunnel. Mainlined. Scott had been more careful since totaling his last truck, his *baby*, so I had no worries letting him keep his keys. We tooled through the tunnel of corn, past pole barns and rented-out farmhouses. The truck whined as Scott pushed it up toward seventy miles per hour. It was a downsize from his 2500, but the crash had tapped him out. He stretched his unemployment check to keep oil and gas in the S-10 and even got a used Kenwood sound system he bought off Craigslist. He said he was saving up for an upgrade, but I doubted he had put anything away. He kept a picture taped to his dashboard. It was of me and him sitting in the bed of his 2500. In it, we're both shirtless and holding beers. I don't remember when it was taken.

I rolled down my window and fished a cigarette from my shirt pocket. I wedged it into the gap of my missing teeth and just held it there, spinning it with my tongue.

"Those'll kill ya," he said with a smile. I lit it and inhaled.

"Yeah, or at the very least, leave me without a job," I said.

"Damn right. Those things are a fire hazard, you know?" That guy really knew how to get a laugh out of a body, and we were nearly in tears as we sped toward Owendale Draught.

Scott shouldered his way into the bar. I flicked a butt into the parking lot and followed. Mud from our boots trailed behind us. For a moment, I thought to kick my boots off at the door before I entered, but Scott was already flagging down the bartender. The wood at the bar had "Jamaica" carved into it followed by a few other scars added by later patrons. I read what each one said, listing things or people that "Jamaica" would do. Scott sat and pushed a full glass at me.

"Drink up," he said. "You know the rules: two pitchers and we're out."

I took the beer, Busch Light again, and spun away from the bar. Owendale Draught was one of those places where the walls were more interesting than the people and that was saying a lot. The owner lived down in Florida, I think, or the Carolinas, and he let his cousin Brett run the place. Brett was a self-taught taxidermist and the entire bar was his showroom. He filled it with coyotes and badgers with glinting marble eyes and polished teeth. Crows and owls sat on high wall mounts. Whitetail antlers hung over the bar. On the back wall above the pool tables, Brett mounted the bust of a bull moose. The thing was so big that its nose hovered over the pool tables. It was always in the way. Nobody could play a decent game because of it, so Brett used the tables like any other, setting out cold cuts and slices of white bread for the evening crowd. At the time, the empty areas across the Thumb were breeding grounds for tweakers, and they used to filter in and out of the building. Every once in a while, one would buy a drink, but more times than not they'd wander out just as aimlessly as they wandered in.

"Yeah," Brett said, "one'a them meth heads went off and attacked my moose. Climbed right up on it, clawing and snarling until the antler there snapped off."

"Jesus," Scott said.

"What then?" I asked.

"What do you mean, 'what then?' I jumped over the bar, took the antler, and beat that freako until nobody'd recognize him."

"Like hell you did," I said.

"Like hell I didn't. That project took me the better part of a year to finish. I'll be damned if anyone's getting away with jacking it up."

"That didn't fix your moose, though," I said.

"Don't be stupid," Scott said. "You can't fix something until you get rid of what's breaking it. Right, B?"

"That's the winning answer," Brett said. He poured us two shots, slapped the bar, and walked away to admire the lopsided trophy.

It wasn't hard to believe when you looked at Brett. He fit right in with his trophies: His beard exploded off his face, and it looked like he'd never met a barber he'd liked. His size kept most interactions from escalating, and there is no telling what a man will do on any given day, especially if someone messes with his stuff. Plus, there weren't any tweakers around that night, so maybe Brett did scare them off. The new flat screen had the Tigers game on; they were winning by then. The farmhand crowd had already gone home, and the night folk filtered in.

The first pitcher was going down easy. Scott about smashed his spit glass when the intro to "Sweet Home Alabama" picked through the speakers. I was talking to a couple flies at the end of the bar, two guys I used to pitch against in high school. I don't remember their names and probably didn't know them at the time. All I remembered was that they couldn't hit a slider for shit, the real-big-swing-and-a-miss types.

The front door opened, and a man held it there. He was about our age, not too far past thirty, in crisp, stone-washed jeans and a bright green dress shirt.

"Right this way, ladies," he said as two women ducked under his arm and into the place.

"What in God's name is Mark Sterling doing here?" I said. I nudged

Scott in his side, but when I turned to see if Scott had heard me, I saw he'd gone pale. He looked as if the Pope had caught him carving his name at the bottom of the cross.

Mark was somewhat of a local who's who. Had sold the farm his dad left him to a corporation and done some fancy tax dance to keep most of the cash in his pockets. Every year during deer season, he'd fund some new competition for area hunters, and not just for tagging the biggest buck. He'd come up with challenges for the best built deer blind, best maintained feed plot—hell, he sometimes created photo contests, challenging shutterbugs to capture images that he'd send off to *Outdoor Magazine* and *Field & Stream*. What's more, the awards he gave out were worth it. Before he died, Walter McKinnon won a grand for best tree stand. Mark was also the only person I knew of who'd completed the Run twice in one night, but that had been almost ten years prior. He'd retired a legend after that.

"And whose he got with him?" Scott added. I recognized Chelsea, another high school classmate who'd stuck around. She was wearing a Detroit hoodie and had a ponytail coming out the back of a Tigers hat. I didn't know the redhead sitting with her, though. The two found a table in the corner as Mark approached the bar.

"Look at this. Dick Finney and Scott Butcher." He saw us and clapped his hands together. "I'd love to say I'm surprised to see you here, but I suppose we are who we are." He laughed and waved down Brett. Back in high school, Mark had been the closest thing to a friend that Scott had, besides me. He had played ball with us, but I couldn't remember which position.

"Who are they?" Scott said. He cleared his throat and scooted his stool away from Mark. He pointed with his glass and had his eyebrow arched to the top of his head almost. "Your dates?"

"That's Chelsea Owens and her cousin, Maggie," Mark said. He stared at the ladies a moment too long, then gave us a wink.

"Out of towners." Scott said. I was sure that Scott, a farmer of grudges, was pretending not to know her. "Who are they?"

"Well, Dick remembers Chelsea," Mark said. "And Maggie is my fiancée!" Scott swallowed his beer wrong and almost choked. I whistled.

"Mr. Bachelor getting hitched?" I said.

"We ain't in a rush," Mark said. "Why don't you two come watch the rest of the game with us?"

"Can't," Scott said. "We're on the Run." Mark furrowed his brow and looked over at me. I shrugged and raised my glass in cheers.

"That's a tall order," Mark said. "Let me buy the second round."

"You're a good man," Scott said. When the beer came, Mark wished us luck for the rest of the night. He slapped my shoulder and he patted Scott on the thigh, letting his hand rest.

"Good to see you boys," he said. He took his pitcher off to the ladies. "I even got a chilled glass for you, Sweets," I heard him say to his fiancée before I lost them to the noise of the crowd. They waved to us and I returned it.

"Imagine being able to just buy anyone a round," I said.

"That's what you get for selling out," Scott said. He was staring at the pool table of cold cuts and licking his lips. "He got a life of money, but now somebody owns him." Scott was not the kind of guy to show that he was impressed with something. He was a jealous man but, hell, life cost money and Mark had it. I knew Scott knew that.

"What kind of name is *Sweets*?" he added.

"A sweet one," I said. "Eh?" I mimicked a rim shot but Scott wasn't laughing.

"Never thought he'd get married," he mumbled. He downed his beer and ordered a shot.

Dead animals framed the TV, and you couldn't see the right edge of the screen for sake of a beaver's tail. A crowd of early twenty-somethings edged around us, their eyes and beers glinting in the LCD light. Scott loved baseball. Seemed to have his heart and temper tied to every pitch. During our junior year, he lost his starting spot at shortstop to a freshman. He didn't show up to practice for two weeks and when he finally did, he gut punched the coach. I watched the whole thing from the mound. Now, though, it was like the game wasn't even on. Scott had gotten real quiet, and when the bar erupted on a double play, he slinked off to the bathroom without so much as a smile.

My phone had been buzzing most of the night with ignored messages from Amber. I flipped it open and called her.

"Did you listen to my voicemails?" was how she answered the phone.

"Did you have anything new to tell me?" I said.

"You haven't called that Realtor and I don't know why."

"The house isn't fully packed yet."

"You've already used that excuse, Dick."

"Not an excuse if it's true," I said. More folks filed in from outside. I looked at the clock on the wall, almost nine. The Run was young but looked like it would be a big one by the time the night was over.

"Where are you?"

"I'm on the Run," I said. I heard her groan on the other side. "What?"

"There's a place for you here if you get your shit together," Amber said.

"Rachel said she *might* be able to put me in touch with a construction crew," I said. "That's not that same as an actual job."

"Jesus, Dick," Amber said. "That's just how people talk. There's work here for you." Then she hung up.

I think, now that I've had the time to do so, that was the most straightforward thing I heard that night. But I was good at coming up with sound arguments that, to me, laid out every reason I couldn't leave. Not yet, then.

Brett was reorganizing stuffed squirrels behind the bar when a man sat beside me in Scott's stool.

"Someone's sitting there," I said.

"I know," the man said, "I am." I wasn't there to start anything and besides, Scott would be back in a second and the man would move then. Also, my beer was cold and I wanted to enjoy it instead of jawing at some stranger. More people came in and filled the bar.

Scott weaved his way through everyone back toward me.

"What's going on here?" he asked, pointing at the man.

"I told him," I said. I grabbed Scott's half beer from in front of the stranger and handed it back to Scott.

"Shit, man," Scott said, "is it too much to ask for a place to sit while you drink?" I scooted over as far as I could but the stools on my other side were filled. Scott tried wedging himself into the tiny gap I'd made. Someone had fed the jukebox and dance music cranked from the speakers. The place sounded like the bastard child of a nursery rhyme and a bad dream.

"Let's just pound these and get the hell out of here," I said over the humming speakers.

"Screw that," he yelled. "I came here to drink and I want to sit to do that." He backed himself up a little until the stranger shoved him away.

"Hey, fella," the guy said, "stop pushing up on me. I ain't like that." He eyed Scott, gauged him, figured that, like me, he had better things to worry about, and turned back to his drink. Once his lips met the beer, Scott slammed the guy's head forward. The crack of his teeth on glass stood my hair on end and beer spilled across the bar. The stranger spun around and puffed his chest into Scott's. It was like a scene out of a campy western movie, two trail hands squaring off over a scratch of land. I leaned in toward Scott, telling him that we should just go, but he shrugged me off.

"Nah, Dick," he said, "can't leave now. Mr. Up-On-Me wants to dance." He leaned into the stranger.

"Ok, that's enough." Brett swung around the edge of the bar and speared between the men. "Either kiss and make up or get out."

Scott's bald head flushed like a warning light as he tried to muscle past the bartender.

"C'mon," he said reaching for the stranger, "what do you mean 'ain't like that,' huh? You calling me queer?"

"You said it," the man said with a laugh.

I tried coaxing Scott to the door but he pulled from my grasp and lunged toward the stranger. Brett got his arms around Scott's neck and threw him down.

"That's it, man," Brett said, "you're outta here." They tangled until Scott was out the door. I threw a twenty on the bar and ran after them. Outside, Scott was in the dirt and the folks beside me at the door were laughing. I pushed them aside and helped Scott to his feet, corralling him to the truck as he flipped the bird to the crowd.

"Those guys were dicks," he said. He kicked a chunk of gravel toward the side of the building and spat. "Who do they think they are, anyway? I was minding my own business in there."

"C'mon, man," I said. "Let's just get out of here. It's pretty late and I have stuff to do tomorrow, anyway."

"Oh no," he said, "I ain't going anywhere until I have my second pitcher." He turned to me. "Those are the rules. Remember?" He looked like a fish someone had laid out on a dock and forgotten about, his breath heaving his chest in and out of himself. "Two pitchers per place," he continued, "and then we run to the next spot."

"Well, it looks like we're gonna have to skip this one," I said. "It's not like we're the ones who bought it, anyway." Cars sped down the road and the wind pushed the smell of cows up my nose.

"Like hell I'm skipping," Scott said. He stepped toward me and spat again. "What's with you, Dick?"

"Nothing's with me," I said. "You just ran your mouth off again and botched things up. Now let's just go."

"Since when did you become such a pussy?" He forced a finger into my chest. I slapped it away and thought about the last time my dad had ever gotten mad at me. I was sixteen and taller than he was by that time and had just gotten busted for taking his car to go hot-rodding with Scott. As my dad pointed up at me and threatened to take my driving privileges away, I broke down laughing thinking about how powerful he had seemed when I was little. Now, with Scott gazing up at me, I felt the farthest from a laugh I had ever been.

"Dude," he pushed my shoulder, "get your ass back in there and get that pitcher." His eyes had started to glaze over, and he began cracking his neck. I knew that look, knew not to tempt it. I punched the guy once and broke three fingers when I caught his forehead. There are only two kinds of people you can get away with punching: a complete stranger and your best friend. The first because they don't matter and the second because you know they will forgive you the first time. With Scott, I'd learned it wasn't worth it.

Back inside the bar, I got Mark's attention and gave him a ten to buy us another pitcher.

"Keep your money," he said. "A man grieving a parent shouldn't have to buy his own beer. I would know."

"Thanks," I said. Mark hadn't been at the funeral, but Ma's obituary was in the *Advertiser* and nothing gets overlooked in a paper that small. Amber had written it; she was always better with words than me. *Saw the heights people could reach even at their lowest points*, was a line that stuck with me.

"You know," Mark said when he came back with the beer, "if you're looking for a change of pace, you're welcome to stay and watch the game with us. Chelsea just got divorced. You two could commiserate."

"Already told you, Scott and I are—"

"Yeah, yeah," he said, waving me off. "The Run. Woo-hoo. You realize that everyone in here now sees you two as basically the same? Every year brings in more people who don't know you, him, like I do."

"Your point?"

"Scott Butcher will tie you to a reputation that'll suffocate you," he said. "Especially in this neck of the woods."

"I guess you'd know about good reputations," I said. I sipped the beer straight from the pitcher. Mark scrunched his nose and looked as if I'd burped in his face.

"Are you too dumb to see that I'm trying to help you?" he said.

I told him I didn't need help with what people thought of me. He scoffed and ducked through the crowd, back to his dates. That really got me heated. The hell did he mean by that? I didn't care what every year brought. We hadn't changed and if people had a problem with it, it was because they were different, not us. I flirted with the idea of loitering by a corner table with the pitcher, nabbing a sandwich, waiting for a time to slip out unnoticed. But it would be easier to get the chore over with: get the beer, get outside, down it, and get gone. And that's what I did. By the time Brett knew what was up, I was backing the S-10 out and Scott had thrown the empty pitcher into the bed.

"Souvenir," he yelled as we fishtailed our way toward Colwood.

———

The road sign said: *Colwood: Please Reduce Speed*. No actual speed limit, no highway sign. Just a suggestion, a passing thought pinned to the side of the road for people to ignore. I must've been up near seventy when I blew past it. The bar barely sat off the side of the road, a small spot with green steel walls. On the side of it, someone had painted a giant martini glass with a naked woman swimming in it. I didn't know a single person who dared order a martini that far out.

The place was packed, and I had to wedge Scott's truck half in the gravel and half in a cornfield. We heard the music blaring as we climbed the steps of the smoking patio they had built off the side door. I could smell the fresh weather seal and sap bleeding from the knots in the boards. Scott was past drunk. Me, not so much, but he had a way of making those he was close to feel how he was feeling. If he laughed at a joke that someone would never tell their mother, they wound up laughing as if it had been their mother who had been the one who told it. If he cussed out the umps, folks screamed at the TV too, even if they were cheering for the other team. My dad died just before I graduated, cancer, and, yeah, I cried. But a year later, after Scott's mom passed, when I looked across the coffin as they lowered it and saw Scott, wet-faced, red, pinching the corners of his eyes, I fucking lost it. Bawled like a child lost at the fair. Hell, Scott could pull a "Goddamn" from a nun if he'd ever gone to church.

We slid past a couple smokers on the patio. Scott swiped a gob from his lips and threw it over the railing. He wiped his hand on his jeans as he blew through the door. I stayed out and pulled my last smoke from its crumpled pack. People mulled around the parking lot and cars whipped down the road, horns and voices wailing. I leaned on the railing and lit up. Inhaling, I looked out past the gravel lot and the stretch of road. Past the miles of eye-high corn and out toward the towering rows of new cell towers. Ma spent her last years damning those beasts. She convinced herself they warmed the surface of the earth and melted the polar ice caps. Three hundred feet of metal looming out over where pine forests once stood. Their warning lights blinking in time like hundreds of snipers aiming at the horizon. The tip of my cigarette burned orange, calling out over the miles to those warning lights. "I can do that, too," it seemed to say. "I can aim at tomorrow." I pulled hard, making the orange burn to red. I held my breath and flicked the butt out toward those towers and exhaled, imagining that my breath could push the spinning piece of foam a little farther.

The door crashed open and Scott barreled out onto the patio, almost falling down the stairs before steadying himself.

"Dude, Dick." He swung around putting his hands on my shoulders.

"What?" I smelled soggy chew coming from him and knew he had already ordered the first round. He looked like a man dying of thirst who had just stolen a bottle of water.

"Girls, dude."

"What?"

"Girls! You know, sugar, spice, everything nice." He squeezed his chest like he was practicing for those inside. "Let's go, man. I opened your tab and got them a couple drinks. We're all set."

I looked past him toward the road. More horns sounded. More people yelled. Headlights came and went.

"C'mon man, it'll take our minds off stuff." He wrapped an arm around me and pushed me through the door.

———

Colwood was small and that made it seem more crowded. A group hovered by the jukebox. The place was going deaf to some pop song. Waitresses in jeans and cowboy hats wove around sticky tables and dancing mobs. A few big fellas at the bar chanted, "'Merica. 'Merica," as one chugged a beer. An old fly huddled at a corner table, trying to drink through the storm. It reminded me of those nights downstate with Amber and how she'd have to all but drag me from place to place. I pushed through it all, behind Scott, until we got to a table where two younger women in Michigan State hoodies sat palming their beers.

"Ladies, this is Dick," Scott said. "Dick, this is Jennifer and her sister, Paisley." I waved and sat down across from the two kids. And by kids, I mean just that. No way they were twenty-one. Colwood was the place to be if you were young. I was nineteen the first time they served me. I didn't recognize anyone in the crowd now.

We babied that first round but Scott couldn't drink at their pace. He fiddled with his empty glass when I was only halfway through mine. I wasn't feeling much like drinking by that time. Paisley had her nose in her phone. It was one of the smartphones I'd seen advertised. Around the bar, I realized that a lot of the kids had them out, recording each other drinking, huddling for photos. Occasionally, someone would have a disposable camera, like for a bachelor party or something, but that night it seemed like every stupid thing was photo worthy. The flashes made me dizzy, so I tried to keep my focus on our table. Scott cuddled up next

to Jennifer and had his arm around her. The two of them laughed at the
people swaying on the dance floor and yelled at the umpires running
the Tigers game. They were losing by then and Scott was pretty upset. He
kept his spit glass close, and every few minutes, he'd unwrap his arm from
Jennifer and reach for it. Paisley cringed once when she caught him spit.
Her tongue unfolded past her lips as she stared back at her phone. I tried
talking to her about the bullshit that people talk about when they will
never see each other again but she wasn't biting.

"Warm spring."

"Yeah."

"From around here?"

"Yeah."

"Going to college?"

"In the fall." One of those kinds of chats that make you pine for a
kick in the face. She had what I call one of those thousand-inch stares.
You know, one of those kids who convinced themselves that they had
seen every unbearable horror a life could run into. She was no older than
twenty, so I had my doubts.

"I need a smoke," she said to her phone screen. She pushed her beer
away and walked off. I looked over at Scott and Jennifer. She was watching
the people and Scott was staring right into me. A line went up between
us, and I knew he was saying, *Get out of my way with this.* I was out of
smokes and Paisley offered no objection to me following her out.

"Bum one?" I asked. She pulled a pack of Malibu 120s from her pocket
and I immediately regretted asking, but I took one anyway, wedging it
into the gap in my teeth. I looked like a kid sucking on a McDonald's
straw. We didn't say much.

"So Jennifer is your older sister?"

"Younger," she said. "I told your friend that half a dozen times."

"He must've heard wrong," I said.

"I think he just heard what he wanted to," she said. Cars parked along
the shoulders of the road. I wondered where they were all going to fit and
if the bar was going to burst from the people pumping into it. She looked
me over, up and down, and laughed her kid laugh. I'd been laughed at a

lot in my life but, unlike Scott, it didn't bother me too much. I was a lot older than Paisley, so I felt a bit ridiculous. Maybe Mark was kinda onto something. Paisley probably thought that Scott and I were one and the same. She was pretty, that's for sure, and I bet she'd had her fill of every type of guy trying to cozy up to her, and I'd have double downed on betting that she was sick of it.

"So, you start college next semester." I pointed at her shirt. "State, eh? Go Green!" She blew a raspberry.

"State wasn't far enough. This is just a shirt." She rolled the tip of her Malibu on the railing until it came to a burning point. She leaned back, balancing the cigarette between her fingers like she was some kind of black-and-white movie star.

"Oh, well I was gonna say that I used to bomb around down there. Lots of people. Lots of drinking."

"So, exactly like here." She sat up on the railing and waved her arms across the scene. She was right. There were more people at the bar than lived in the village proper, and I didn't know any of them. This was somebody else's idea of fun.

Scott fell out through the door but pulled himself upright next to me.

"What's that smell?" he asked. He looked at me smoking. "Dude, you're smoking a lady cig. Where'd you get that?" He slapped his knee and spit onto the wood.

"Where's Jennifer?" I asked.

"Who? Oh, yeah. Taking a piss," he said. "She's . . ." he smiled, biting his bottom lip. Paisley saw that from over the edge of her phone and snorted.

"Something to say?" he asked her. Sweat beaded at the top of his head.

"No," she said to her phone.

"No, no," Scott said, "you've got something to say. I can tell. I can always tell when someone's got something to say." He looked back at me. "I can smell it." He looked convinced that he was going to prove something. Once in East Lansing, a frat boy kept pestering Amber for her number. We were already back to just friends by then, but we agreed that when needed, I'd be called on to be her buffer. She'd place a hand high on my thigh and that was enough to keep the mosquitoes away. Warding off polo shirt assholes also wasn't my idea of fun, and though Scott didn't look the part, he was acting it.

"'Lady cig,' huh?" Paisley said. She pulled on her Malibu. "And you even know what they smell like. Got something you're not telling your friend?" She twitched her head toward me.

I go back sometimes, to when Scott and I were juniors, to that time he punched our coach as I watched from the pitcher's mound. I remember seeing him walk up to the coach, like he was going to apologize for skipping practice. He stood there, nodding while the coach harped at him. Something clicked in Scott then, and I can still see it: His eyes glazed over and he popped that guy a good one. Just like that.

I don't blame that girl for what she said, can't really blame her for anything now. She must have thought that the glaze over Scott's eyes was just all the beer. When Scott slugged our coach, I had just stood and watched. Laughed a little even; the guy was a right prick anyway. But as that girl eyed Scott with more disgust than someone would give a beggar, I tried to stop him. Or at least hold him up. He was quicker than me, though, and his fist snapped out and cracked that girl on the side of her head, right by her eye, and she flew backward over the railing.

I pushed Scott away from her, looking over my shoulder. A gasp came from her, as if she were drowning in air. She crumpled into a pile on the gravel below and started convulsing, a streak of blood crawling from the corner of her eye. Someone screamed and ran into the bar. Cellphones that one second were capturing pictures of people blowing smoke rings were pointed at us, their lights flashing, illuminating me and Scott as we leaned over the railing, looking at what had happened. A moment later, Jennifer ran through the door along with a wash of people. She clawed through the crowd and when she saw her sister, she screamed one of those screams that I don't know how to forget. Some guys pulled Scott into the growing mob, a few good shots landed on him, and he just took them, staring at where Paisley had been sitting.

The mob pulled the two of us apart. I took a fist in the teeth, and I was taught that if somebody was swinging for you, you best be swinging back. I punched at no one in particular and called out to Scott. The 'Merica guys had him pinned against the steel siding but he wasn't fighting back. I remember falling to the floor and a knee in my back pinning me down. They pushed me against the railing, my face pressed between two wooden supports, and I was forced to look down at Paisley. Foam bubbled from her mouth and soaked her hoodie. More cameras flashed. Some cars and trucks peeled out from the lot, sending chunks of gravel flying into the sides of those that remained. State trooper lights stretched from down the road and sirens sang out. A mass of people ran everywhere and nowhere.

An ambulance took Paisley away and two state cruisers took Scott and me. It took the county ten whole months just to set a court date for my disorderly, didn't matter that I was defending myself. I guess Paisley was an epileptic and when news came that she died on the ride to Caro Community Hospital, the court pushed Scott through the system, booking to confession to sentencing, before the month was out. I don't think Scott knew what was happening until he was pleading guilty. Part of me believes that he believed if he just cooperated, they'd go easy on him. This wasn't Hollywood, though—no anger management and a swat to the back of the thighs. They saw Scott's three DUIs, the crash, my missing teeth, and the suspicion surrounding the lumberyard in his history and gave him a full fifteen years. Boom. Just like that.

When I got out of holding, I went to Ma's place and someone had spray-painted KILLER across her front door. Two windows had been smashed in and the gutters all around it had been ripped down and left hanging in the wind. I called Amber to tell her the news, but she already knew everything.

"Did you think I was too far away to learn what you did?" she said. "It's 2009, Richard, everyone and everything is a text away."

"I didn't do anything," I said.

"That's not how folks see it," was the last thing she said to me.

Tuscola County's jail was overcrowded so they struck a deal with Saginaw County and hauled Scott's ass an hour away to their correctional facility. I stayed away for a long time. I told myself it was because I had my own stuff to worry about, the court and the fines, Ma's stuff, whether it was worth it to repair the house. Stories grew out of that night, and

I still hear rumblings from time to time. The one that sticks the most is the one where I held Paisley like a punching bag for Scott. What it really came down to was that I was afraid to see Scott, to see him locked away, there but not really there. I didn't know what I would say if I saw him.

The sugar beet season came to an end and so did my job. When I picked up my last paycheck, my boss told me that Pioneer didn't want me back the next year. Not having a job lined up pushes a person to make some hard choices, and I paid one of those buy-and-sell eBay places to help me dole out Ma's stuff. They took 20 percent. It wasn't until after I gutted her place and listed it that I got around to seeing Scott. Every time I went, he'd press the phone on the other side of the glass hard to his ear like he was afraid that whatever I said would blow away before it got to him. He never mentioned Paisley, and I didn't bring her up. He assured me that he'd be out early for good behavior. I couldn't bring myself to tell him that left us closer to forty than thirty years old. I just smiled and told him I'd be back in a few weeks to see him.

I only kept that up for a year.

———

Then Scott was involved in some kind of "incident," and they moved him from Saginaw down to the big prison in Jackson, a good three hours and a hundred bucks in gas away. I had a job stocking shelves at Walmart and ran into his dad there not too long after. He said Scott was a "person of interest" surrounding whatever happened, and that it was all just a big, unfortunate mistake. I'd had my fill of those and didn't ask any further.

The last time I did see Scott was the only trip I ended up taking downstate. It was his thirty-second birthday, and I brought him a small cake. He had been downstate for about nine months by then. I hadn't written him in a while, and I didn't want to go empty-handed. I felt pretty dumb bringing a cake to a prison. I expected the guards to cut into it to see if I had baked a metal file into it or something. It's funny how a life runs down so many back roads over its course just to be boiled down to having an old friend bring you a cake while you're locked up. Like it was all just part of a corny movie I'd seen too many times.

It's funny. It has to be. I'm just trying to remember to laugh at it.

I sat at a metal table and watched Scott inhale half of that cake before either one of us said anything more than "hello." He had fallen into himself by then, like an empty pack of cigarettes. He was growing his hair out but it was thin like corn silk. He kept dipping his tongue behind his bottom lip as if there were still chew wedged in there. Muscle memory. I tried to think of something that might cheer him up.

"I've been thinking," I said.

"Yeah?"

"When you get out of here, maybe we could start the Run right where we left off."

"Why would you want to do that?" He ran a finger along his gum line and to me he looked like he'd hooked onto a phantom wad of Kodiak. He'd become small in his white prison jumpsuit, his skin as thin as frost and his lips stained blue with cake frosting.

"Why not?"

Scott grunted. "Don't think I'll be in much shape for running whenever I get out."

"So that's it? You're going to throw away your future because of your past?"

"Look, Dick, I'm here for the long haul. You're not."

"Scott, you understand that folks back home think I'm just as guilty as you? I'm not as free as you think I am."

"Then why don't you move?" He sucked frosting off his thumb and smiled. "Getting out of the Thumb is good for a person. In here, I get to be who I want to be. I couldn't do that back home." I remember looking away from him then, up at the clock mounted behind a clock-sized cage on the wall. I resented him, then, for thinking he left as a choice and then had the nerve to say he'd grown.

"Well," I leaned back, motioning for the guard to end our time together. I pushed the remnants of the cake toward him. "Guess I best be getting out of here. Beat the traffic."

———

Colwood closed last summer. I drove up there a few weeks ago, just to see what was left. Dandelions caulked the cracks near the building, and someone spray-painted a giant red mustache on the girl in the martini glass. I parked on the far end of the lot and got out. Someone had put up one of those roadside memorials in the corner of the field, the kind that family members erect at the scene of an accident. It wasn't much, two lengths of weather-treated two-by-fours nailed together like a cross. It used to say *Paisley*, but the sun and wind had faded the letters so all it said was *Pa—y*. I grabbed Ma's urn from the passenger seat and walked over to the memorial and set her down next to it.

"Hey, Paisley," I said. Her name punched me in the chest and I could barely breathe. She'd have long graduated from college by then, had she not run into Scott, into me. Hell, she could have easily been halfway to having her own little girl old enough to hear stories of her mother conquering the Run. Maybe they would have lived in a townhouse in Chicago and the daughter would have thought the stories of the backwoods were as far away and mesmerizing as the moon. Until that night, I was happy living in the Thumb, thought that it had everything, but I couldn't blame people for wanting to get out, to go far away. I thought of the people I'd known in high school who had faraway plans for their lives. Large parts of me hated them, not for leaving, but for being the types of people who could stay gone, who could make a go and hang around in places where count-less lives sped along, around, and into each other. I hated them for being the types of people who could survive the crashes. None of the ones who left ever came back.

Amber had cultivated a new world with new possibilities on the far side of Lake Michigan. I couldn't even keep up in a college town. Hell, in a bastard way, even Scott left. I opened Ma's jar and laid some of her ashes under the cross, to keep Paisley company, then went back to my car. I plopped back in my seat and sat there staring west. A new energy firm had recently won a bid to build a wind farm, and a handful of turbines were already up on the horizon. They loom over everything, and when I do get the nerve to sit in a bar, nobody is complaining about cell towers anymore. They pass around smartphones, trying to get each other to read articles about turbines causing cancer or blogs describing the best way to sabotage them. People left, and in the vacuum, the world came knocking at our front door. Its pounding keeps me up at night.

About the Lies

I changed my name to Jamaica after the death of my father, Wallace Southby, salt truck driver for Tuscola County, golfer, and lover of craft beer and crafty women who weren't my mother. That was two years ago. Now I'm living in a one-bedroom apartment above a hair salon in Caro, Michigan, the same one I've been in since my divorce almost eight years ago. Before that, I was Mrs. Brent Garret, and before that, I was the only person I'd ever been, Miss Amy Southby, pronounced "SUHT-bee."

My father would not have approved of my newest name.

———

It was one of those mornings where the corners of my eyes felt like burnt pie crust. I woke up with a man sleeping next to me and, for the life of me, I couldn't remember his name. I knew what had happened the night before. I've never been that far gone. He was one of the field hands or grease monkeys that came into Owendale Draught with half their pay-checks set aside for MGD and a burger. He wasn't a regular but came in enough that I sort of recognized him. He'd sat down at the bar sometime after the early birds cashed out. It was my birthday, the name-iversary of Jamaica, so I gave him to me, a present.

But I hadn't gotten his name along with his body, and I felt a tinge of shame at the oversight. I let him sleep, though, wrapped in a sheet, with my favorite pillow wedged between his thighs. I propped my back against the headboard and watched him. The skin on his face and forearms was the dull, all-over tan of a man who only came indoors to take a shower and change into new work clothes. He smelled sharp, like mint body wash, and for a moment, when he pulled the sheet up under his chin and grumbled in some dream, I saw a resemblance of every man I ever knew in how he moved his lips.

The things I'd collected over the course of my life were treasures, and my favorite pieces I displayed in my bedroom. Every summer during the town's Cars and Crafts fair, I found one thing to bring home. One year, I'd bought a floor lamp someone had welded to resemble an ivy vine reaching upward; some of the leaves made shelves. Another year, I watched an old man whittle tiny cowboy boots. He told me they were supposed to be toothpick holders. I brought three home for the ivy shelves. This year, a girl was selling airbrush portraits she fit onto index cards. I pinned mine to the wall by the lamp. Used books and a stack of trade magazines lined the floor moldings across from the bed. I liked to read about cars—only a small part of that came from my ex-husband, most of it was because I wanted to know how to fix what I was driving. I filled the walls with photos I found at estate sales of people that I had never met. The only new things I owned were the glass coffee table in the living room and my queen bed. I'd bought them together on sale. The man snored in the middle of my little museum, and maybe it was just the headache and nausea playing tricks on me, but I felt, so help me, comfortable with that man.

It was quarter to eleven. I'd stayed in bed longer than I usually did, trying to remember his name, until I had to use the restroom. With the door cracked, I washed my face and checked my teeth in the mirror. I'd forgotten to brush the night before and a shift's worth of beer caked the inside of my mouth. I brushed, peed, and tossed my hair through my fingers. I popped a Tylenol and fished for the half pack of cigarettes I swore were still in the medicine cabinet. They were gone, which meant I'd have to bother the girls downstairs for a few. The man had sprawled across to my side of the bed. I let him alone. I wouldn't be gone for long.

———

Colleen's Beauty School is the oldest salon in Caro, and the string of salons across town, all run by her graduates, I think is a testament to the woman's work. Though if anyone asked her, which they shouldn't, she'd spend the whole appointment grumbling about betrayal and bottom lines while she tugged scalp and neglected to put a rolled towel over the edge of the sink. The we'll-go-to-church-next-week crowd was in and the chairs were filled with women I knew by face, not name.

"Back already?" Colleen said. "I just started here. Bridgette could take you," she pointed down the aisle with her comb.

"On the back half of a cut and color," Bridgette said. "Could rotate you in if a trim is all you need."

"Just need a couple smokes," I said. Colleen, her hands full of bright red hair, twisted her hips away from the chair, keeping her eyes on the woman she was working with. I pulled a pack from her apron.

"Dye?" I asked the woman Colleen was working on. I'd never seen hair so red.

"Natural," the woman said. I didn't know her, but she was gorgeous, at least I thought so. The bridge of her nose fanning up into a brow she'd scrunched up as she read *People*. Ears pushed forward just enough to make them poke from her hair. Short, her chair pumped higher than the other women.

"Lucky," I said. I pulled three smokes and put them in my pocket. I held up a fourth like a question.

"Go ahead," Colleen said. "I'll put that one on your rent."

"Your first drink is on me," I said. I rolled it between my fingers, sticking it up like a thin middle finger before lipping it. I grabbed a copy of the Sunday *Advertiser* sitting on a chair in the waiting area.

"Are you going to smoke that in here?" the redhead asked.

"Of course not," I said. "I've got a better spot."

———

I swear the cars on Sunday mornings are quieter than any other time of the week. My window opens out over State Street, and every week the cars sound like a rolling breeze. I sit in that window and listen to the singing church bells and it seems like the whole damn countryside is calling out to one another, crying out the name of the Lord. I saw a cellphone commercial once and when it showed the company's coverage map, there was the Thumb, grayed out, forgotten. My father used to say that to the rest of the country, we were nobodies but to each other—he held up his right hand, Michigan's Lower Peninsula, and pointed to the middle of his thumb, where the skin wrinkled at the knuckle, where we lived—he'd say at least we were Thumbodies. He loved that pun. When those church bells let loose, I can only agree with him. *Thank you, sugar beets*, they'd call out if bells were voices. *Thank you, family. Thank you, bad GPAs, dead ends, and contentment with twenty grand a year. Thank you. Thank you. Thank you!* I don't go to church. I get enough from hearing those bells.

I was into my second cigarette when the bedroom door opened. The man leaned onto the doorjamb in only his jeans. The white V-neck from the night before tucked into his back pocket like a deer's tail.

"Morning," he said.

I blew smoke out the window and picked a speck of something off the tip of my tongue. "Good morning," I said.

"Can I use your facilities?" he asked. My *facilities*. As if he were renting out space in a boardinghouse or were a TV repairman on the job. But at least he had that Midwestern politeness that people around here used when they went shopping, or were on the phone with customer service, or, apparently, when they woke up in a bartender's' apartment. When he was done, he leaned across me, still shirtless, and stuck his head out the window. That close, I could zero in on the line where his pale skin burned into his tan. He was so white he almost looked blue. His smell was stronger now, the breeze from the window giving it more life. He smelled like a worker, like a body that didn't know what to do with itself if it sat around too long. He smelled like a Jeff or a Cal.

He hunched his shoulders a bit, growled up some phlegm, and spit out the window before pulling himself back in.

"I used a fingerful of your toothpaste," he said. "I hope that isn't a problem."

"No, not at all," I said. "Want a smoke?" I wasn't ready to make a pot of coffee just yet and I felt like I needed to offer the guy something.

"Thanks," he said, taking one. He held it between his finger and his thumb and pulled the length of it below his nose, breathing it in like a man at a cigar shop. "Good roll," he said. He winked and laughed. It was a small laugh but enough to pull one from me. He leaned against the wall, sliding down until he reached the floor. He was tall, his head over the sill with a sightline straight up my shorts. If he saw me, he wasn't showing it. This Jeff or Cal seemed like the kind of guy who played things cool like that. I finished my cigarette and flicked the butt to the street below. I picked the newspaper up from the floor and opened it.

"What's the good news?" he asked.

"No idea," I said. "I start with the letters to the editor." They were my favorite part of the paper, especially in the big Sunday edition. I loved how the polite format hid some real petty shit. They were like precursors to internet comment sections, but even better because I loved seeing how long the writer had held onto their beef with either a previous week's article or, better yet, another letter that they desperately wanted to trash. I already got all the news I needed off my phone, anyway. I read one to him about a wind turbine farm that had gone up east of town. The writer had addressed their letter "To Any Logical Thinker" and gone on in great detail about how the spinning shadows from the turbines killed migratory birds and drove people insane. It ended with a call to arms "to stand against the BIG WIND lobbyists at all costs."

"Sounds like a guy I used to know," Maybe-Jeff-or-Cal said. "Old drinking buddy of mine. Kinda stupid but he's not exactly wrong."

I folded down the edge of the paper. "Excuse me?" I said. "More like *not exactly right*."

"The jury's out," he said. "I see that same guy from time to time and he swears those things gave him insomnia." He pulled at his long eyelashes, rubbing sleep from them. He was wrong, of course, dead wrong, but I wasn't going to throw him out because he said something ignorant.

"I bet you that you're wrong," I said. He twisted a finger at the corner of his eye then blinked quickly, looking up at me.

"What's your wager?" he asked.

"A haircut," I said. He snorted at this but ran a hand through his hair, leaving deep, sweaty furrows along the side. "You need one, anyway."

"Ouch," he said. "I usually just buzz it when it gets bad."

"If you win, then you can do just that," I said. "But when I win, we go downstairs and get you one at Colleen's."

"How about if I win, we go back to bed?" he pushed up with his elbows from the windowsill and kissed my knee. That sounded like a win for both of us, but still, I already had my phone opened to an article.

"Read," I said. He scrolled, reading slowly, mouthing the words silently, shooting his eyebrows up every so often.

"*Twenty-five peer-reviewed studies have found that living near wind turbines does not pose a risk on human health*," he read.

"This is just one article, though," he said. I leaned over him and tapped the hyperlink in what he'd just read. I messed with his hair as he read on.

"I think you have enough here for a pomp fade," I said, kissing his ear.

"What's 'peer-reviewed?'" he said.

"You know when your car won't start and you don't know why, so you call your buddies over; one says battery, other says alternator, and eventually you all figure it out? That's peer-reviewed, except all the buddies are mechanics."

"And there's twenty-five of them."

"In just one article," I said. "In the vast sea of the internet."

"Dang," he said, handing the phone back. "I was wrong." Three magical words and I could've taken him there on the living room floor, but that would've blurred the lines between who was right and who had lost.

"Put your shirt on," I said. "You're gonna look great."

———

"You're not getting any more cigarettes," Colleen said. She was sweeping her station, bright red curls piled at the bottom of the chair. The place had emptied out and I heard the other stylists talking from beyond the back door. The redhead was gone, too, and I was a little upset I'd missed the extra chance to see her.

"You'll give me one if I ask extra nice," I said. I led Maybe-Jeff-or-Cal by his shoulders to the empty chair. "I also brought NEW business. That's gotta count toward something." I pushed him down. "Pomp and fade and a wash," I said.

"I didn't agree to that," the man said.

"Colleen here is the best in town," I said. "You're going to look great." I leaned down and whispered into his ear, "You lost but you also kinda won." I winked at him and parked myself in the chair next to him.

"When was the last time you washed your hair?" Colleen said to the man. She tossed a cloth around him, cinching it around his neck. He didn't say anything, but blush ran across his face.

"I'm sorry," he finally said. "I sweat a lot at my job."

"What do you do?" I asked. Colleen leaned him backward into the sink and I couldn't hear his response over the water.

I met Brent in a math course at Delta Community College. It was hard not to notice him. I sat behind him, and he had a head of hair that made him a good three inches taller. I pestered him to switch me spots and he offered on the condition we study together. I agreed and after a few failed study sessions, the last of which started with the transitive property and ended with his head between my thighs, we started going steady.

Brent was gorgeous but not exactly smart. He didn't see himself as college material. I took to it fine enough but found that I wasn't giving the classes the attention they needed. At the time, I would say I'd rather have spent my days with Brent. Which is what I started doing more than going to class. The truth was being the daughter of a dead seasonal county worker didn't exactly give me the financial cushion needed to see myself making it even to an associate's degree. I could barely afford the first semester, so where was the money for another three going to come from? Despite acing my classes up until midterms, it just didn't make sense to pour my time into pretending the money was going to just appear. I may not have a degree, but I know what a sunk-cost fallacy is.

Brent and I married not long after we both dropped out, and like most things that come out of turning your back on one thing for another, it stopped being fun and exciting once the newness of it flew away. What I started feeling for Brent became an angry love that most people call resentment, and as soon as he gave his name to me, I wanted to give it back.

I bounced between waitressing jobs until I was given a chance behind the bar up in Colwood. When that place got shut down, I bounced around more until I wound up at Owendale Draught. Brent spent most of his time at his uncle's garage an hour away in Saginaw. We became two pay- checks to one another, paying our half of the rent for close to three years.

Maybe-Jeff-or-Cal leaned into the salon's mirror and whistled.

"Right?" I said. He pulled a fifty from his wallet and told Colleen to keep the change.

"I was wrong to doubt you," he said. There were the three magic words again. We made it as far as my couch before I pushed him down and straddled his lap. He was thin but strong and I could make out the line on his chest where his ribs bowed outward from his sternum. The skin of his torso was younger than the rest of him, than his arms and face. Now, shirtless and his warm hands on my hips, he looked like a patchwork with a father's head and arms attached to a son's body. A science project of generations.

After, I lay on top of him, and we shared my last cigarette.

"Big place for just one body," he said.

"I fill it pretty well," I said. He pointed to a framed photo of a little girl hanging on the wall above the couch.

"Your little one?" he asked. In the photo, the girl was wedged in the Y of a maple tree. It was fall and she had a spectrum of red, yellow, and orange leaves wrapped in her arms. The girl was young, very, and smiling the way a child who just learned how to smile does, showing as many teeth as possible because that's what they were told to do when someone took their picture. I found it in a cardboard box labeled "ten cents" at a garage sale in Owendale.

"No, that's a photo of me." I knew that a four-by-six photo of a little blonde girl didn't matter in the grand plan of post-orgasm small talk. And because I don't have any memories of playing in leaves. I took the cigarette from his lips and pushed myself from him, letting my fingertips graze his knee.

"Coffee?" I asked. Before he could answer, I was around the corner pulling the Folgers from the cupboard.

"Sounds perfect," he said. Then as if it were related to morning coffee, as if the two subjects couldn't be talked about in any other way than together, he asked, "So, no kids?"

———

Mrs. Brent Garret was a lie, and I was Mrs. Brent Garret. The transitive property of an unknown identity and gone like so many words whispered under bedsheets. The divorce was short and the sweetest thing for both of us. There wasn't anything to split, really. Just a handshake. I think I signed one thing as "Amy Garret-Southby" after that, but it seemed too formal, too mechanical. Plus, I've always thought that a hyphen in a name was a sign of somebody who didn't really know who they were. A person who wanted to make everyone in their life, present or gone, recognized and happy. By the time I would have been graduating with a bachelor's degree, all I had was a divorce and the need to pay a full rent check every month.

———

I listened to the gurgling coffee and thought of the best answer I could give the man on my couch. I didn't want to have kids, didn't want to pass anything of me on to them. The bad or the good. Before meeting my father, my mother was married to a soybean farmer from Unionville, a man who spent most of his time in his combine jerking it to wrinkled liquor store pornos. Then she tied herself to my father, and I washed in less than a year later.

When I was seventeen, Mom left when she learned Dad had been getting too comfy with one of the secretaries at the county clerk's office. Just to keep even with him, Mom bought a bunch of black leather pants and torn jeans then started running with the bassist of a Flint bar band. She sure knew how to pick them, and since she was half of me and my father was the other half, I bet they passed on some pedigreed life-choice-making-skills. Brent and Maybe-Jeff-or-Cal were proof of that.

I wondered who I'd be if my mother's first husband had made up the other half of me. No worse off than now, just a different kind of worse off, I suppose. Maybe if I'd have been a boy, I'd be the one sitting in a woman's apartment, drinking her coffee. I didn't want kids because I didn't want to give them that, the pieces of a human being that you don't have control over. I could tell the man that I'd tried, once, when Brent and I spent the times we weren't at work wrapped in each other on any flat surface. Even that couch he was sitting on. But this seemed like a shorter if not better answer:

"Nope," I said. "Cream? Sugar?"

"Sugar," he said. "Four spoons."

We split the rest of the coffee and I sat down on the other side of the couch. We'd spent the last part of the afternoon in safe small talk. I told him I graduated from Caro High in '04. He from Cass City in '00, which made him older than I thought. Made the patchwork of his body seem more stark, sad almost. We laughed over how some kids climbed onto the Caro water tower and painted it so it looked like a giant, blue breast hovering over the north end of town. He found pictures of it on his phone, and we laughed harder with each swipe.

"This is embarrassing," he said, "and I'm sorry, but I can't for the life of me remember your name." He began to fuss with his hair, but I pulled his hand away. I could have asked him his name then, but it would have ruined him, that comfort that he had with me, here, in the home of a person he'd never been with, a person he only knew in the guiltiest of ways.

I'd heard a song about a girl named Jamaica, back when people still knew me as Amy. In the song, a man sang about this girl he once knew, a girl who the singer had wanted to stay with no matter where life took them. It made me think that was who I wanted to be, a woman that people wanted to have stay with them, the decision to stay or leave all hers. The song ended with the singer watching Jamaica leave him as she sailed away from port on some vague idea of discovery. And as she goes, he continues talking to her, as if she were sitting right next to him, whispering to her the plans he had for the two of them, not caring, possibly not knowing, that she couldn't hear him.

An incoming call flashed on his phone with a zoomed-in picture of a woman and the name "Sweets" across her forehead. He jumped up from the couch and closed the bedroom door behind him. He mumbled an answer and I only made out every other word or so. He was supposed to be somewhere, I gathered, and was late. I took the mug to the sink letting the water run so I couldn't hear the man and Sweets anymore. Was this who I was? Not the woman a man wanted to have come back, but a vacation to escape to?

Maybe-Jeff-or-Cal came out of my room, in shirt and socks, still talking.

"No, Sweets," he said, "I told you. I had a few too many and slept in the truck." He came up behind me and kissed me on the cheek. His lips were cold and it made my teeth hurt. "No," he continued, "I haven't been to Owendale in months. I met Tim at the Oasis." He placed his hand on mine, the one rinsing his mug. "Yes," he continued, "I can do a late lunch. Where?" Sweets named a place I'd never heard of. Her voice was sharp and clear. She was gorgeous, I could tell. He took the mug. Our hands had turned under the faucet and water bubbled over the mug's rim, pelting the bottom of the metal sink. He downed it then refilled it. Before hanging up, he promised to meet her soon.

I shut off the water and came around the corner. The man eased into his spot, sipping his water. He winked at me and I wanted to hate him for it, for his lie. Hate him for the way he kissed me while still on the phone and for the pastiness of his goddamn chest and the beautiful wrinkles in the corners of his eyes that made him look like he'd seen enough of life to know better. I sat on my end of the couch and pulled my knees up to my chest, folding my arms in front of them. I rested my chin on them and glared at him.

"Where were we?" He asked. *We*, he said. Together.

"Your wife?" I asked. I pointed to his phone.

"Not yet."

"But soon?"

"Does it matter?" He stopped smiling and I didn't know the right answer. Did it matter? I was there, with him, hauling around the touches and breaths and words we'd shared, but I wasn't attached. I could make it not matter just as easily as he had, but that would have left me the only kid without a chair to sit in when the music stopped.

—

I was still Amy, a senior captain on the golf team, when Mr. Elms, the high school economics teacher and my coach, kissed me after I had sunk a thirty-foot eagle putt on a par five at the Caro Community Golf Course. He was a new teacher, and though I told everyone at the time—my teammates, my parents, the principal, the police—that he had been the kisser and I the kissed, the truth, the fact was that when I sent that ball on its way across the green, when the echoed *twock* of the putter against the ball had faded and I watched the little white dot roll easily, lovingly toward the cup, I knew I had wanted him to. Confident that the ball would sink and that Mr. Elms would congratulate me. Married to the fact that when he gave me his high five, the one he offered all the girls when they chipped like a pro or split a drive down the fairway, that I'd hold onto his hand just a little too long, smile with just a little too much teeth and a little too much "yes, you can, yes, I'll let you" shining in my eyes. Knowing that would be all the two of us needed.

There was a fuzzy area of wrongness in that kiss but nothing criminal. That wrongness scared me, though, pulled me back into the child that eighteen-year-olds still are. So, I told on Mr. Elms, and once the words were to the winds, I wanted them back, wanted to clutch them in my teeth, swallow them down and have them warm me from the bank of memories kept in my guts. It was easy for the school to let Mr. Elms go. The teachers' union couldn't save him, not that they had wanted to. I was eighteen when it happened, and in the eyes of the Tuscola County prosecutor, nothing sexually illegal had happened. For that, I was thankful. None of that mattered to Mr. Elms, though.

He was only twenty-six at the time. Three years younger than I am now.

Before this, there had been talk of a scholarship for me. Even the coaches from places like Vanderbilt and Michigan came out to play rounds with me. After that kiss, though, it all stopped. The school had to forfeit the rest of the season because the team didn't have a coach and nobody wanted to take up the role. The recruiters caught wind of the situation and they stopped visiting. That stung for a little while, but by the time I would have been competing in regionals, I had lost my desire for the game. I played some weekends with my dad, but mostly I'd show up to the clubhouse after class and walk the links alone. I graduated with a 2.2 grade point average and no university suitors. I had woken up early the first Saturday after graduation and paid for eighteen holes. My opening drive was perfect, a straight bomb with enough topspin to send the ball rolling for another fifty yards after it landed. A year before, I would have thought it was more than perfect; it would have been gorgeous. I would have felt that drive inside me like how a child feels when they pour out all their Halloween candy and start to archive their haul. But I felt nothing. It was simply mechanical perfection, the kind of thing you expect to see on a car assembly line. I holstered my club, stuffed my glove into my back pocket, and walked back to the clubhouse, leaving my bag in the first hole's tee box. I'm sure someone nabbed them that same day.

———

"I'm a state-ranked golfer," I said. "Or, I used to be." A reactionary memory. I wanted to say something that could keep up with people who brunched.

"That's cool," Maybe-Jeff-or-Cal said. He strummed his fingers on the couch arm and shifted in his seat. "I play a little, when I have time."

"No, you don't understand," I moved closer to him. "People came all the way out here to play with me. I'm telling you, I was great."

"Do you still play?"

"Hell yeah," I lied. I thought of the tips I made that week. The men weren't coming in from the fields as much as they used to. I had barely enough for rent let alone a round of golf.

"Maybe we could get out one of these days," he said. He looked toward the window and though I knew this was how small talk ended, I wanted to stay with him in our lies, little and big. Who knows, maybe if we did golf together, I'd leave a lasting impression on him.

"I'd like that," I said. His phone chimed and he groaned at a text.

"Look, uh," he started. He straightened himself.

"Yes, right," I said. I got up from the couch and he followed me to the door. We hugged the kind of goodbye hug you give a second cousin when they come to your high school graduation.

"So, I'll call you," he said, but I didn't remember giving him my number. And then he was gone with the front door already tight in its jamb.

I locked it and sat on my sill, looking down to the street. It was like any other day now, as if church had never happened. The sounds of duallys and motorcycles and life filled the streets. The bells were done and I didn't hear any *thank-yous*. Maybe-Jeff-or-Cal came out onto the sidewalk.

"What's your name?" I called down to him. He looked up to me and squinted. "Your name," I yelled. I should have had the nerve to ask him when he was on my couch, should have had the gall to tell him I didn't remember. He pointed at his ear then turned his palms up and shook his head. Through that distance I realized that he was drifting off to somewhere I could never go.

———

It had been a long shift and I loved it. It was December and college kids were home for break, some trying to tackle the cross-county bar crawl

they called the Run. It was like this every winter, and it was the best time
for me to rake in some extra cash. My car needed new tires, and a couple
more nights like the one I was having would leave me with plenty left
over for something fun. I'd been thinking about golf more often since my
morning with Maybe-Jeff-or-Cal and had thoughts toward a new set of
clubs. Wads of folded fives and singles bulged my apron, and by the time
one person left, two more had already taken their place.

A man and woman sat down in a small hole in the middle of the bar,
and before they had their winter gear off, I laid coasters out for them.

"Happy Saturday," I said. My eyes were down the bar watching an old
farmer flirt with one of my waitresses. I was going to cut him off after
his next drink.

"Happy Saturday," the man said. The voice made my eardrums swell,
and it felt like someone had just started a round of horseshoes in my head.
It was Maybe-Jeff-or-Cal with a fresh haircut, the same style we'd gotten
him that summer. Had it not been for the woman he was with, he'd have
had my full attention. But I knew her, by face, not name. She was the
woman from the salon. Jesus Christ, from the same chair, even. Her red
hair still curled as if she'd never come out from under Colleen's hands.

"Happy Saturday," she said. She sat, stretching her back. I wasn't on her
mind, wasn't even a blip. Just the bartender.

I tossed a towel over my shoulder and asked them what they were
having.

"Bud," Maybe-Jeff-or-Cal said. "What'll you have, Sweets?"

"Absolut and tonic," she said. She folded her scarf on the seat of the
stool and tucked her gloves into her hat. She was pale, with light makeup
to make her more so, and it looked as if she were trying to be a blank
canvas with only red spilled on her. I wasn't the only one staring. Most
of the men at the bar swayed back and forth on their stools to see her,
and I wondered if she knew this was how the world acted with her in it.
Maybe-Jeff-or-Cal, though, watched me pour their drinks.

"I was thinking," Sweets said, leaning into him, "the bar at our wedding
should have *His & Hers* cocktails."

"We haven't even set a date," Maybe-Jeff-or-Cal said.

"Yet," Sweets said.

"If you don't marry her, I will," a man called from down the bar. A few others by the taps whistled, and I slapped the bar in front of them. One geezer apologized, but by the looks on their faces, the couple enjoyed the attention. I brought the drinks and asked if they wanted to start a tab.

"I've got cash," he said. He handed me a ten and a five and told me to keep the change.

"Been a long time since I've been here," Sweets said.

"Me too," he said. And then they were lost in the sound of the rest of the world. A waitress spilled a tray of empty glasses, and I left to find the broom.

I came back and scanned the glasses on the bar for refills. Maybe-Jeff-or-Cal had mostly ignored his beer. Sweets was talking to him as much with her eyes as with her mouth. He nodded and nodded some more as her eyes and lips spread. It must have been a doozy of a story. I stopped in front of them.

"How are we doing here?" I asked.

"Order me another one, Mark. Okay?" She ran her hand across his shoulders and made for the restrooms.

"Fancy seeing you here," he said. He tried to smile but it was a chore for him. I busied myself with making the drink. "Maggie wanted to meet a few friends but they bailed. It was going to be a girl's night." I put her drink on a coaster and started washing pint glasses. He had half a beer, but I dumped it anyway and washed it. He began to protest but only got so far as to hang his mouth open and think of something better. "She turned twenty-one here," he added. "She wanted to get the girls together. Sort of a nostalgia, ten-year anniversary thing. I wasn't originally going to come. I mean that. She was set on coming. I'm just here because of her."

"You want another?" I asked.

"Not right now," he said. I walked down the bar and refilled a handful of empties. I worked the register and filled a drink order for a table in the corner. When I came back, Sweets had her stool nestled next to *Mark's* and an arm around his waist.

"Can I get a water?" she asked. Her voice was clear, beautiful. It matched her face and what I had pictured that morning after. I could have told her then. I could have said something like, "Does he stuff your pillow between his legs like he did mine? Do you choke him like I did?" Or just, "Your fiancé came home with me one night last summer. I didn't know about you. I'm sorry."

Was that true? Was I sorry? Who was there to be sorry for? Definitely not me. I had a great time up until she called. Sorry for her? For what she didn't know? If I told her, she could do anything. She could blame me, she could hit me. She could do both of those things to him. She could do both of those things to both of us.

"Miss?" she said. "I know you, don't I?"

"I've lived here all my life," I said. "I like your man's haircut."

"It's different," she said, rubbing the back of his neck. "That's for sure."

Mark had his hands under his thighs now, and I knew he could read my thoughts. He wanted me to keep our lie. He wanted to survive. I felt closer to him then than I had in my bed or on my couch. The sharp kind of closeness that pisses you off with how tired it makes you. But I had him chained to whatever I chose to do.

But then, who, what, did that make me? I'd be a bomb to their life. It could kill them, her. I didn't know if I could live with myself if that happened.

"That's too much ice," Sweets said. "There's barely any water." I slid the drink across to her anyway, pretending not to hear over the crowd. "I can see why you don't come here," she said to him. "The service isn't very good."

I hovered around the ends of the bar, wiping spills and laughing at the things customers said that I hadn't heard or even registered. Beer cans hissed open, and some college kids were singing both the Kingston and Cass City high schools' fight songs. Mark angled himself toward Sweets, but I would catch his attention wandering over to me every time she took a sip or drifted into her phone. He had that stupid cute look on his face again, like a kindergartener sitting in time-out.

The evening pushed on and I racked up a few miles behind the bar. People were loud, moving, happy or trying their best to be. Mark stood and kissed Sweets on the forehead. He headed to the bathroom, back straight, watching me in his peripheral.

Sweets pulled an ice cube from her glass and chewed on it. She held up a finger, calling me over.

"Can I get another drink?" Of course, she could get another drink. She could have two if she wanted them. I felt like I owed her that at least.

"Anything else?" I asked.

"I'm all set."

"Hey, Jamaica," a regular called. She waved to me from down the bar. "Can I get an Arrow and tonic?"

"Jamaica?" Sweets asked. "That's an odd name. Pretty, though. How'd you get that?" She had a wonderful smile, and the way she tilted her head told me that she was interested but confused. Why Jamaica? Why here? Why me? I had an answer for her, but the story was long and it involved moments that she would not have liked. Her Mark wasn't back from the bathroom yet. The crowd was thick and loud and dying of thirst. Someone fed the jukebox and a couple waitresses danced with customers. I had work to do, a role to play. Still, I wrung the story through my mind and wondered where, if, to start. And which parts, if any, I should leave out.

Her, Guts and All

The agreement started with Rid Bellows Sr. He owned the most plowable earth north of Caro not bought out by a corporate farm: a 700-acre tract of cropland he rotated with corn and soybeans whose northwestern boundary snuggled up along the Cass River. He'd been the first farmer in the county to buy his own crop duster and had flattened out a runway on his property. He'd gotten most of the other landowners around to side with him: There would be no harvesting of a whitetail deer unless it had antlers grown beyond the width of its ears. Levon Cutler had been the first neighbor to agree. He was an Army man and drew a pension that could tide him over through the winters. Plus, shooting does went against his morals. Mark Sterling used to own a small farm farther east, past the river, but soon after taking it over from his father, he leased the 200 acres off to a corporation, using the tax exchange to buy as much forest as the DNR had up for auction. Now he had untouched land to continue with his old man's tradition of hosting an annual deer camp every November. Alton Southby to the north was too old to hunt, so Rid Sr. didn't bother asking him. It was an agreement between men, he decided, and what kind of man didn't hunt?

The last person Rid Sr. needed to speak to about this matter was Sandra McKinnon, Walter McKinnon's widow. She owned a regrettable plot of woods on the opposite bank of the river, the side that eased its way down to the water, unlike his side that sat a good fifteen feet above it. He had known Walter well enough and had hired him on as a farmhand for a few seasons. That man had worked hard, like he was auditioning for a permanent position. But that would have meant putting him on the payroll, and it was easier to pay him weekly with an envelope of cash tucked in the back of his mailbox. That had been almost a decade ago when the recession hit and people needed work and were willing to give it cheap. Now all that was left of Walter McKinnon was his obituary and a couple deteriorating tree stands Rid Sr. could see from his side of the river. A heart attack at forty-two had fought with high blood pressure most his life. Rid Sr.'s wife had mentioned it to him one morning, and he'd responded that the man had worked too hard, too quickly, and was left with little more than nothing to show for it. Some people, Rid Sr. believed, weren't cut out for country living. He'd been tempted to buy the land decades prior, before the McKinnons moved in, but he passed on the idea after walking the property with the Realtor. It was swamped out, in a constant state of sogginess, and Rid Sr. could tell by the gradualness in which it sloped toward the river that it was a flood hazard. The rinky-dink house on the property would have cost him more to keep livable than it would earn him to have rented it out. When the big flood of 1986 came and busted the dam upstream and washed away a handful of homes on that side of the river, he knew he'd made a wise choice.

It was early November when he walked onto the McKinnons' land. There had been a cold rain the night before and a mist hung around that morning. The trees were naked, but the air still held onto the smell of wet firepits used to burn leaves before the snow came. Rid Sr. thought the property smelled like soot and vinegar and it made him think of vomit. He was unused to land smelling like anything but grain dust and fertilizer. His dad had told him that was the smell of growth, and his grandpa had told him it was the smell of success. Having tripled the size of Bellows Farms that was left to him, he believed them to be right. As for the other side of the river, the same old house stood at the end of the long, packed-dirt driveway, and Rid Sr. had to give the McKinnons some credit for keeping the place upright. When he'd first seen the house, it had looked more like a temporary ticket-taker shack outside a traveling circus; any slight breeze might have up and taken it away. Now, though, hunkered behind cedar bushes, with white hardwood smoke churning out of the chimney, it looked as if it belonged on the front end of those small twenty acres. Rid Sr. knocked on the storm door and let himself into the breezeway.

"Hello? Ms. McKinnon, it's Rid Sr." He poked his head through the doorway leading into the kitchen.

Sandra McKinnon met him there. She was in jeans and a too-big flannel. Her black hair hung down the back of her neck in a loose pony-tail and streaks of grease marked her face. She wrung a dirty rag between her hands.

"In the business of letting yourself into other people's homes?" she asked. She tucked the rag into her front pocket.

"I'm sorry," Rid Sr. said. "I knocked. I always came right in when you'd have me over for dinner."

"That was before. What do you want?"

"I'm here with some news from the neighbors. We've all been talking about hunting season, and I was hoping you had a minute so as I could get you abreast of what we've all discussed."

Sandra wiped her forehead with the back of her hand, making a new grease streak to match the rest. "Fine. You should come in, though. I'm in the middle of something." He followed her into the kitchen. "Take off your shoes in the breezeway," she said.

"I won't be here long," he said. He crossed, leaving behind quarter-sized pools of water from his boots. The kitchen was the largest room in the house. It could have easily taken up a third of the entire house. The floor tiles were cracked but clean, and the sink was an old-style ceramic double basin, marked with years of scratches from pans and silverware. In the middle of the room was the table piled with thawing bags of meat, what looked like bread dough, and a gallon of store-brand vanilla ice cream. At the far end of the room, beyond the table, stood a small refrigerator and a chest freezer. The fridge had been pulled from the wall and the freezer angled away from it just enough to allow Sandra to crouch down behind it. Rid Sr. sat at the table.

"What's going on here?" he asked.

"Freezer won't keep temperature. Had to empty it just so I could move it off the wall." The top of her head bobbed behind it and metal clanged every few seconds. "You stupid piece—come on!"

"Do you need help?" He didn't get up from the chair.

"It could be the thermostat. Or the compressor. I'm not sure." She rose from her corner juggling a pair of pliers and a screwdriver in one hand and a small metal box with copper coils in the other. She laid them out on top of the freezer and pulled the rag from her pocket. "That doesn't look broke to me. What about you?"

"They look fine to me."

She climbed from her corner and moved to the coffee maker. "You want some?"

"I would," he said. "Thank you."

She poured a second cup and popped both in the microwave. She turned to Rid Sr. and leaned on the counter. "It ain't old," she said. "The coffee, I mean. It just needs some life zapped into it. I was up at quarter to five messing with the freezer."

"Coffee is coffee," Rid Sr. said. Truth of it was, he enjoyed any kind of coffee he didn't have to make himself. She sat across from him, pushing the ice cream away from between them.

"If it's not the thermostat or the compressor," she said, "then I don't know what it could be."

"What's that mean?"

"Means a lot of spoiled food and a new freezer I can't afford. Curt Sterling is over, maybe he could look at it. He's handy."

"He out hunting with your boy right now? Bow season's got a few days left."

"No, Walt was going to teach him to bow this summer but that of course didn't happen. He and Curt are scoping out a spot to set up a tree stand. Junior found a deer run by the river and has seen about a dozen deer this week."

"Well that's what I wanted to talk to you about." He sipped his coffee.

"I'm listening."

"I'm sixty years old, Sandra. I've filled a lot of tags. Dropped a lot of deer and even missed a few in my day. Same as every hunter in the area. But you know what I haven't tagged?"

"What?"

"The big one. The buck that makes the front page of the paper. That makes people talk. The trophy that makes the entire region look to us and say, 'those folks know what they're doing.'"

Sandra returned to the freezer and grabbed the thermostat, flipping it over in her hand. A new one would only cost her seventy dollars, Rid

Sr. guessed, but the thing looked pristine. "Maybe you're just not lucky enough," she said.

"Been playing too long for luck to have anything to do with it," he said. "No, what I've come to understand is that everyone around here gets themselves a bad case of buck fever every time they see bones on the other side of their shotguns. Don't matter if it's a spike or even a button buck. Folks just line 'em up and bang. Bag and tag and forget the future that deer coulda had."

Sandra disappeared behind the freezer. It was smaller than the ones Rid Sr. had in his garage, but unlike her husband who had been big and had hooked hay without breaking a sweat, she was the kind of person you'd lose in a cornfield if they turned sideways.

"So, what are you telling me?" she said.

"Well, the long and short of it is that I've talked to folks around here and we've all come to an agreement that there won't be any shooting of deer unless they are bucks. And only then, the antlers have to be grown out beyond the spread of the animal's ears." He was looking forward to seeing his home filled with trophy busts mounted on his walls. "Basically, we're only gonna take deer worth taking."

"Who agreed to this?" Sandra poked her head around the freezer, still elbow-deep in its backside.

"Everybody. We talked about it before bow season started." He helped himself to another coffee, turning the microwave dial to ninety seconds. He heard metal scrape against metal and Sandra gasp.

"Goddammit," she said. Something crashed inside the machine and her head shot up. "That was over a month ago."

"We wanted to make sure nobody over-harvested before firearm season started."

"And you thought to only tell me this now? When opening day is less than a week away?"

"Well, I assumed you were, you know, with your husband's passing and all, occupied." He grabbed his coffee and returned to his chair. Sandra wrapped the rag around a bloody thumb.

"What do you think all that meat in front of you is?" she asked. "We don't have beef in our budget. Last year my husband took three deer. My son only got one. That's what's left of all of it."

"I'm sure your husband would have agreed."

"Don't," she said. "You don't get to speak for a dead man, especially my husband. Walt took his tag limit every year and now Junior will have to do the same. Look around you. Where do you think you are? It might not be hundreds of acres of soy or wheat or sugar beets, and it may flood during a wet spring, but make no mistake, Mr. Bellows, you're on solid land. That I own."

"Now listen here," Rid Sr. said. "Do you know how much goes into taking a deer? You've got the license, the shells, the guns, the camo, blind maintenance. Hell, I'm a working man and my time is worth something, too." He drank his coffee long enough to char the back of anyone's throat. "So, you gotta tell yourself, if I'm going to do something, it better be worth it and it better put me out ahead."

"My husband hunted this land for twenty years and the deer he took were what kept us through the winters," Sandra replied.

"But you gotta understand," Rid Sr. said. "There's only so many deer and even less worth taking. If you shoot just anything, they can't grow up to be trophies."

"Worth," she said, air-quoting with the bloody, greasy rag and a screwdriver, "has got as many meanings as there are people alive. You can't eat antlers." Rid Sr. chuckled at this. People like Sandra, he believed, had countless ways of making it look like they were hard up. They had a victim mentality that he found sickening and, considering the way 2016 was ending, enough honest men like himself had had enough of their whining.

"Well, this sure has been fun," he said, "but let me ask you this. Isn't it Levon who comes to plow you out every winter when the storms hit? And don't Mark Sterling rent you a plot of his land every spring to plant your canning vegetables?"

"Your point?"

"Well, this agreement ain't just mine, you know. They have just as much to agree upon in this as I do, as you should, and I'm sure they wouldn't take too keenly on knowing that while they're trying to foster a community, you're hunkered down in your little patch of woods doing everything in your power to unravel the whole thing. Do you understand what I'm saying, Sandra?"

"Mr. Bellows."

"Call me Senior."

"Then call me Ms. McKinnon." The two held each other's names in their teeth, rolling them like jawbreakers.

The back door opened and Walter Jr. and Curt came into the kitchen. Curt could have passed for a smaller clone of his brother, Mark, built to last with knuckles like lug nuts. He had already proven himself to be a reliable farmhand. Walter Jr., on the other hand, took after his mother and looked like he could hardly lift a shotgun let alone level its sights long enough to down a deer.

"Saw five just now, Ma," the boy said. "Two does and three yearlings." He pulled his camo jacket off and looked the room over. "Oh, hello," he said to Rid Sr.

"Hey there, Junior," Rid Sr. said. He put his hand out.

"People call me McKinnon," Walter Jr. said. He shoved his hand into Senior's and shook.

"Seen any signs of monster bucks out there?"

"Only a few scrapes on some saplings and rubs dug into the ground in the thicker brush. Plenty of doe though."

"It looks like from all this meat you're a good shot."

"My dad taught me. That was a four-point I took late last season."

"You don't say. Well that's exactly what I was talking to your mother about."

"Why's all your meat on the table, Sandra?" Curt asked.

"Freezer won't work," she said. She held her thumb under the faucet then wrapped it again.

"Is it the compressor?"

"I wouldn't know."

"Let me take a look at it. I fixed up one for my brother last year."

"I don't think that's a good idea," Rid Sr. said. He put his hand on the boy's shoulder. "Ms. McKinnon here doesn't seem to understand what it means to be a good neighbor. We should treat her accordingly."

"But the food," Curt said.

"No buts, boy. What would your brother say if I told him I wasn't going to hire you out no more? He might've gone corporate but he's still gotta maintain that speck of farmland. How much hide do you think he'd take off you if I refused to dust his crops?"

"That's not fair," the boy said. He shook his head in short jerks, like a puppy who'd licked a lime. Curt was still a sweet kid but if he didn't figure out how life worked out in the country, Rid Sr. was sure Mark would toss his little brother out on his ass, just like Rid Sr. had done to his son.

"That's a word that's got as many meanings as there are people alive," Senior said. He heard Sandra scoff behind him. "Listen, boy, you're a part of this community and being a good citizen means listening to your elders. Don't talk to me about what's fair. Fair is owning a plane and choosing where you fly it. Fair is letting a button buck grow up. Don't confuse fair and equal, boy. Now get gone. The McKinnons don't need your help."

The boy backed out of the kitchen. The storm door slammed and Senior and the McKinnons saw him speed down the driveway on his bicycle.

"Now, son," Senior said, "don't act the fool and let this get past the point where I'll need more than words to get my point across. No does, no nothing but the big one. You hear?" McKinnon said nothing. "I mean it. Both of you. We've got our own little slice of paradise this far out. Don't ruin it. Remember what happened when your daddy tried screwing with the order of things." Sandra moved between Senior and her son.

"Get out of my house, Senior," she said.

"I was already leaving. Now you two have a wonderful day." He let himself out.

"What about the freezer, Mom?" McKinnon asked.

Sandra sat at the table and put a hand on one of the bags, a roast. It was mostly thawed. "C'mon," she said, "let's find a place to store this."

The deep cold came in a week later, on the morning before opening day. When Sandra went out to the Ford Escort she and Walter had shared for their entire marriage, it wouldn't start, no matter how much she pounded on the steering wheel and prayed. The plan was to get a résumé typed up at the library because she did not want to scour Caro's storefronts, offices, and diners empty-handed. She had ironed her only pair of slacks the night before and was hoping that some employer would see her spotty employment over the last fifteen years for what it was: the product of a budget-conscious household manager. Tim Darling's landscape business was growing, maybe he needed an office manager. She still believed Caro was a small town, but she couldn't exactly describe it as tight-knit anymore. *Maybe it never was*, she thought. The election cycle had painted places like the Thumb as left-behind casualties of the recession, but she'd scraped her whole life, Walter too, while people like Rid Sr. made rules that fixed the game. No, Sandra thought, no, there wasn't a lived, us-against-the-world mentality that she'd picked up on in the papers and local news. It was an us-against-ourselves standoff. This damned big buck agreement was proof of that.

The Ford sputtered and finally turned over and Sandra thanked the car gods. Now all she had to do was let the thing warm up. She popped the trunk and fished out a set of new wiper blades. She'd put off replacing them, she hated the hassle, but new blades for the oncoming winter was another chore that at least she could stop juggling.

Her son walked out onto the front porch with a cup of coffee and a piece of toast.

"Got this for you," he said holding out the cup. He popped the toast between his teeth and walked out to her.

"Just hold it for a sec," she said. She pried the blade arm from the frozen windshield and fiddled with the hooking mechanism.

"Senior was pretty bent last week," he said.

"You don't need to worry about that."

"Sounded like the opposite of that."

"And what I just said sounded like exactly what I just said." She twisted the old blade free and tossed it on the ground. She picked up the new one and tried fitting it on the arm.

"Ma, I know about that bull agreement Senior was talking about. Curt told me. It's stupid."

"That's enough, Junior," she said. She pushed the blade but it wouldn't lock into place. "People like Senior believe that their words mean more than others. Most of the time they don't."

"So, what, we just shut up?" he said. "Ma, I'm telling you, we don't need those people but we do need to eat." Sandra admired this can-do, must-do attitude from her son. And he was right, they needed to eat. But there was a difference between talking and doing, and the damn shame of it all was that learning this lesson usually came through failure, something they'd had enough of.

The new wiper blade slipped in her hand, and she almost lost her balance on the slick driveway.

"Stop," she said. "You stop it!" She slammed the wiper blade against the windshield, then again, and again, shouting "stop" every time the rubber hit the glass. The blade had bent and was now useless. Sandra dropped it on the hood and turned, leaning against the small car that Walter had once picked her up in when he wasn't a husband, just a Friday night date. This was supposed to be the last winter with the Escort, but now that Walter was gone, she'd have to figure out a way to keep its tires spinning, especially with Junior only a couple months away from sixteen. "Didn't you hear what Senior said? Do you remember what he did just because your father set up a tree strand too close to the river?"

Junior coming into the world had been the best way to start 2001. But after September of that year? Well, people had a lot of hate they spent the next fifteen years molding into armor. The McKinnons felt they were lucky to be able to cloister in their corner of the woods and get a savings going for Junior's future. They pretended to argue over college or trade school. *Maybe he'll become our little poet,* she'd say to tease Walter. He'd respond by blowing a raspberry and say something like, *No money in writing about deer.* Their savings account wasn't a match for 2008 and Walter began to curse the idea of "savings." *Banks ain't gonna tell you it's not meant as saving for a future. It's saving your ass for the here and now.* They hadn't planned on raising their son in a world so eager to break itself over and over again. But Junior was a solid student and a better son, even if he was a little too eager to please. On weekends, Walter took him along to odd jobs so he could pick up a few practical lessons on how to keep a life going. They were doing fine at keeping theirs going until Walter wasn't.

"I remember you grounded me for walking near the river," Junior said. "Do you want me to get the blades on?"

"I can do it," Sandra said.

"You're doing a bang-up job of it," he said. He smiled with too much teeth and that always made her smile, even if she'd taught him better manners. He got the sarcasm from his father; it was a trait of his she'd grown to love and that feeling doubled onto her son. She sat sideways in the driver's seat, rubbing the back of her neck with her tired, sweaty palm, the same she'd used to swat the back of her son's thighs when he'd needed an attitude adjustment.

"So, you're going out hunting tomorrow?" she asked.

"We need me to," he said. He picked up the wiper blade from the windshield and slid it back into its packaging. "I'm sure we can tell Walmart that it was bent when we bought it. We'll get a new one tomorrow after I come in from the woods."

"Might snow tomorrow. The news said we could get a few inches."

"Then we'll go into town the day after that. We're in no hurry."

She'd been unable to fix the freezer and a repair bill was out of the question, especially if it only resulted in a temporary fix. They'd been forced to keep the food chilled outside, but raccoons had gotten into the ice cream on the first night. It was hard to think of Michigan winter as anything but long and cold, but it wouldn't last forever, an irony Sandra didn't want to live with.

"Not yet," she said.

———

It wasn't his best shot. He'd missed the heart and maybe only grazed a lung. "A runner," his dad would have called it—a shot that would eventually kill the animal, though it would take a few hundred yards before it knew there was no outrunning what was chasing it. It was amazing how perfectly the doe crossed the river, like a knife across a whetstone. She seemed to glide across the surface of the water, avoiding the deep hole dredged by the current where McKinnon's dad had taught him how to fish. Before the echo of the shot could fade into a buzz in his ear, the doe was already in the tree line on the opposite bank. Its tail was down, a good sign. McKinnon knew it couldn't run much farther before its strength bled out of the hole he'd just shot into it.

Then it hit him. The doe had run onto Senior's property.

"No, no, no," McKinnon said. He set his safety and slung the shotgun over his shoulder. He climbed down from his stand so fast that had his father been around to see him, he'd have gotten an earful for being so careless. He ran through the brush to where he'd made contact. A small amount of blood had pooled but there was no blowout splatter that would've let him know he'd fully hit the doe's vitals. McKinnon followed where the doe had run, blood every few yards, marking where her hooves had hit the mud and her heart had pumped out of the wound. He couldn't see any corn or chewed vegetation, signs that would've shown he'd completely botched it and gut-shot the poor thing. When he got to the river, McKinnon found a large red pool on the bank, washing down into the slow current. She was dead, she just didn't know it yet. McKinnon squinted out to the other side of the river, a narrow tree line at the top of a ten-foot drop-off on the opposite bank, and hoped she'd figured it out by now.

It had happened so quickly. McKinnon had no idea how much time had passed between him taking the shot and him now standing at the water's edge. He paced his side of the river, trying to keep away from the rotting stilts that were all that remained of his dad's blind. He'd helped his dad build that blind, as much as a nine-year-old could help raise a sixteen-foot stand. He mostly held the tools and weather seal.

It had been a great blind. It even won an award put on by one of the rich neighbors. Mr. Sterling had given McKinnon's dad a plaque made from deer antlers that said Best Blind 2010. It was probably still up there, the points on the antlers gnawed down by squirrels. Or maybe it was still intact. McKinnon had never been allowed inside. That year, McKinnon's dad had busted into the house on opening day having only been out for an hour. He looked scared, something McKinnon had never seen in his father. His mother kept asking and asking what was wrong until he told them.

He'd barely settled into the stand when a hole blasted through the plywood wall above him. Then another. He'd fallen backward and almost completely out of the stand and to the ground when he'd heard a shotgun's echo. Then came the yelling and the swearing. "The hell you doing, man?" It had been Rid Sr. standing on his side of the river, pointing a shotgun across the water. "You hunting my land?" McKinnon's dad had been shaking as he told his story. It didn't matter that the stand was obviously on McKinnon land. "Don't matter," Rid Sr. had said, "you're still aiming out onto my land." They'd called the sheriff, but he was an old township board friend of Senior's and the complaint died before it made it off the property. Since then, McKinnon had been strictly forbidden from being anywhere near the river during whitetail season.

A half mile up was Bucky's Bridge. He could cross there and climb down to the opposite bank. But that would be half a mile of trespassing and then he'd have the doe's carcass to haul back. He walked back to where she had crossed. The river was shallow, even the fishing hole was no more than a couple feet deep. He'd dragged deer through the swamp on the north side of the property before, had cut his way with his gutting knife through tangled brush while getting deer out to a clearing to field dress them in relative ease. He could probably get a deer across a shallow river, he thought. Why not? He stepped into the water. He'd gotten a new pair of rubber boots the previous Christmas and they rose halfway up his calves. As long as he watched where he stepped, he could stay dry. He took a second step then looked down at himself. From the waist up, he was nothing but blaze orange, a flag in the middle of a drab forest. He ran back up on the bank and stuffed his coat in the Y of an ash tree as a marker to help him get back.

He returned to the water, stepped in, and slid each step forward, not raising his feet too far off the rocky bottom. He was afraid of slipping and having his 12-gauge fall into the river, so he held it tightly against his chest with both hands. His dad would have beat his butt raw had he known his boy was doing what he was doing but every man, every woman, hell even every fifteen-year-old boy had a claim to what they paid for, and McKinnon knew that doe was rightfully his. He'd get to the other side of the Cass River, get the doe, and get home safe before dark. He'd hang her in the shed just in case Senior or one of the neighbors snooped as they drove past the house. It was a perfect plan and soon after he'd laid it out, McKinnon was on Senior's side of the river. Some water had splashed over the tops of his boots and he could feel his wool socks sticking to his feet. He repositioned his shotgun onto his shoulder and pulled a foot out of his boot, took the sock off, and wrung out what water he could before putting it back on. It started to snow while he worked on his second sock.

He found where the doe had clamored up through the brush, blood streaking the bark of an ash tree and dotting the ground. What people measured in feet deer seemed to measure in inches, and the steep bank took that doe only a couple large leaps to scale. McKinnon made his way up slowly, bracing himself against stumps to push himself upward. He didn't see a body at the top of the bank, but as he inched closer to the farm field up ahead, he finally saw her just past the tree line lying in a fold of dirt, her head propped up on a clod of tilled earth. His heart swelled in his throat. It was forty yards out in the open, in perfect view of three tree lines. McKinnon crouched down at his line behind a row of logged hardwood. It looked as if Senior and his men had split it the season before and that didn't sit well with McKinnon. It meant that he wasn't sneaking onto a forgotten corner of Senior's land. He was trespassing right in the middle of it.

He'd have to be quick and careful.

Across the river, his coat was a speck of orange barely visible through the falling snow. He could see it only because he knew where to look for it. Opposite the field, though, McKinnon had no idea who might have eyes on the doe. He scanned the trees for any trace of human life. Any orange would be a clear giveaway, and, if they were out there, whoever they were, they'd have seen the doe come busting through the cover into the field. Certainly they were waiting for whomever shot it to attempt to come and claim it. He remembered seeing the holes blown into the walls of his dad's stand when he helped him tear it down.

McKinnon felt hunted in those moments when he searched for another hunter. The snow fell in large, heavy flakes, and in the quiet of it all, he could hear them as they fell against the branches and along the ground. They sounded like thousands of pencils on notebook paper.

Senior had been madder than any man McKinnon had ever known

when his mother told him off the week before. He felt that from any point along the stretches of trees and scrubs some angry SOB might have a barrel pointing right at that doe waiting to fire. McKinnon regretted bringing his gun along then. He was already trespassing, but now he was armed and Senior could make up any number of excuses to fire. Maybe he'd told his family and anyone else hunting his property about his run-in with the mother and son across the river. Surely, he'd told them about the agreement. How many eyes were out there, watching, waiting? McKinnon had lingered on that final thought long enough for half an inch of snow to fall. The doe's body was still warm, and snow melted as it hit its tan fur. It stood out in the white.

A wind had come in and he was glad his father had taught him the proper way to layer his clothing to keep out the coldest drafts. But his socks were damp and the crouching was keeping his blood from flowing properly. He felt pins shooting into the tips of his toes and knew he had to act soon.

"Get moving," he told himself. "Move your feet." He said it in a way that he'd remembered his father saying it, urgent but playful, as if he were happy to have a son to inconvenience him from time to time. He took in the trees one last time then he went. He kept low and moved slowly to the body. He could grab her by the hind legs, drag her to the trees, and field dress her by the river. He would be able to kick her insides into the water and they'd be gone, the snow would cover his tracks and any remaining blood. Nobody would know he'd been on the property. Nobody would know that he'd broken the agreement.

From behind the log pile, the field had looked like a slab of uneven concrete, but McKinnon sank in mud with each step. He was ankle-deep when he came up next to the body. His footprints dotted the snow behind him like brown exclamation points signaling his arrival.

She was bigger than he had thought she was. It was something that his father said never happened. "They all look big between the sights but not up close." McKinnon assumed she'd be around 120 pounds and would dress out to just over ninety. She would be manageable enough to smuggle back home. But this time, McKinnon's father's advice had been wrong, and the doe at his feet was easily fifty or sixty pounds larger. In fact, it was one of the largest deer the boy had ever shot, and having that realization made him want to cry. He bent over the body and placed a hand on her side. She was barely warm and had collapsed with the bullet's exit wound facing up. He ran his hand up to her shoulder, the fur ruffling and falling back into place. His shot had missed a good chunk of vitals. The slug had torn away the fur and left a dark red, almost black, burn just behind the front leg. She'd suffered only for a short time but still too much.

A shotgun blast called across the field and sent McKinnon belly down into the mud beside the deer. It had happened, he thought. Senior had spotted him and was going to see to it that the punk kid next door learned a lesson impossible to forget. A second shot followed, but now that McKinnon had an ear to the distance, he realized that it was farther up the field, closer to the front of the Bellows' land. Peeking over the body, he saw half a dozen deer running back toward the river. They were a hundred yards away, out of any sensible person's range. That settled him. The snow was starting to accumulate on the doe's carcass; it was after four and the daylight wouldn't last much longer. McKinnon knew whoever had shot would be eager to get their trophy.

About seventy yards up, a patch of orange came through the trees. It had to be Senior; nobody else was with him. The hunter moved quickly in the opposite direction of McKinnon. There was every chance that they'd have seen him but the figure didn't look back as it followed the trajectory of the other deer. As soon as the hunter hit the trees, McKinnon was on his feet, tugging at the doe's hind legs.

The mud hadn't frozen, not even close, and he couldn't get a solid footing between where he'd been and where he wanted to be. He dragged the doe, stopping every few yards to catch his breath and readjust the load. The bright side, he told himself, was that he'd be able to stretch the meat of a deer this size for weeks. And, despite the trees and the river, he was less than one hundred yards from home.

McKinnon got to the log pile and dropped the carcass behind it. He needed to rest, to gather his wits. The last thing he, or his mother for that matter, wanted was for him to be too tired to get across the river. The current had taken a handful of lives in its day. Kids would hold their breaths when the school bus crossed Bucky's Bridge, believing that Bucky's ghost haunted the waters below the road. McKinnon did not want to become another story. He grabbed a log from the pile, dusted the snow off, and used it for a chair. He laughed. He was going to pull it off. Senior could talk all he wanted, a big man walking into folks' homes thinking he had something to say worth hearing and thinking he'd be able to enforce whatever nonsense he spouted. Rich folks, McKinnon thought, they could get like that when there were people like him and his mother to boss around. He had been raised in a world like that, and he especially knew it to be true in Caro, where land was worth more on the high side of the river, where those who had less could only afford to live where nature threatened to kill them during every spring thaw. *Fuck Mr. Ridley Bellows Sr.*, McKinnon thought. What better way to make him shove it than to not only survive but to get away with living.

He shivered. The wind had finally cut into him now that he'd worked up a sweat. He rose from the log and turned toward the river to see a flash of orange only a dozen yards upriver. It was Senior for sure. McKinnon could make out every gray hair on his temples. He was standing over a buck, of course he was, and he had already gotten it open, its innards hanging out over the open side of its chest cavity. McKinnon hunkered against the log pile and watched as his neighbor cut the body free from itself. Senior worked quickly, too, quicker than anyone McKinnon had seen, and in less than ten minutes, Senior was walking back up the riverbank, leaving the buck in the snow. No way he'd work himself to death getting that carcass back up to his barn, McKinnon thought. The old man was going to grab a tractor or more likely a four-wheeler to do the heavy lifting for him.

That meant McKinnon had less time than he wanted to field dress his doe and get her home. Had she been as small as he'd thought, he would have entertained the stupidity of hauling her, guts and all, across the Cass. The burden of his own dumb luck hit him again and the tears burned the corners of his eyes. He wished his dad were there to yell at him. He'd be mad, sure, but at least he'd be there to help.

McKinnon snapped out of it and grabbed the deer by the legs again. He pulled her to the edge of the bank and she slid down to the water's edge. He got over her and spread her back legs. She was starting to go stiff and it was getting darker. McKinnon had gutted enough deer to know the steps, but never in the dark and never anywhere other than the safety of his own woods. He grabbed the soft white fur around her teats and pushed the knife into the skin. The knife was sharp, and the skin pulled apart easily as he drew the blade up like a zipper on a coat. The white-blue of the skin spread, revealing the faded green-purple of her intestines. He stopped before he got to her stomach and pocketed the knife. Her legs wouldn't stay open, and he needed to break her hips to allow himself more room to work. He stepped on one hind leg and pulled the other out as far as it would go before stepping down on it. He gathered his balance then shot his weight downward onto her bones. She cracked easily and on the second stomp, she broke. McKinnon got the knife and knelt back down. He grabbed at the open edge of skin to restart. His eyes were trying to adjust to the dark and when he found where he'd left off, he sunk the knife back in. He heard a soft pop then.

"Oh no," he whispered. He lifted the knife barely half a centimeter and cut upward, revealing his mistake. He'd punctured the stomach. Chunky green bile oozed out of the small opening in the stomach, the pressure of which forced the hole to tear and more gunk spilled out. Then came the smell of rotten grass, bile, vomit, and corn, and McKinnon forgot then about being cold. The only thing he thought about was maintaining, about keeping his own stomach from purging itself. He couldn't stand and do the job correctly, he had to be there, close, inside of it all to do it properly. He took a breath and dove in. The blade reached the ribs and he forced it into the sternum. A thick layer of fat covered the bones. The blade progressed in half-inch stretches. Ten inches past the stomach, McKinnon stopped. There was blood, a lot of it, covering the liver and the lungs. He found the heart, or half of it anyway. So he had nailed it, dead on, after all. She had run so far, though, without a heart, crossed an entire river and scaled its high bank just looking for a place where she could be safe. Maybe she was on her way home when McKinnon had zeroed in on her and she thought that if she gave it enough oomph she could get there and everything would be all right, that she wouldn't die that day, surely not in the middle of a muddy field.

In the distance, Senior cranked on his four-wheeler. He had the choke on all the way and was letting it warm up. McKinnon only had a handful of minutes left.

He cut the remains of the heart out and laid it off to the side. He reached up into the chest and pressed the knife into the esophagus then down the spine. Every few inches he cupped a handful of organs and pulled them away from his work. He lost his footing when he heard Senior kick the four-wheeler into gear, his entire left arm falling into the slop that spilled from the stomach.

"Damn," he said. He wiped himself on the doe's fur, she'd wash in the river anyway, and went back to work cutting the organs free from the abdomen. Senior's four-wheeler started its way back to the river. In a minute, he'd be right on top of McKinnon, and McKinnon didn't want to know what might happen then. When he'd made his way back down the doe's body, he pressed the knife into the groin and used all his weight to crack the pelvis. He tucked his knife away and squatted down, sliding his hands under the doe's body. He lifted her and rolled her stomach down into the Cass, letting what had kept her alive fall out of her. The four-wheeler's lights rippled through the trees, and by the time Senior reached the top of the bank, McKinnon was halfway home, river water flooding into his boots.

On his property, McKinnon dragged the doe until his legs and lungs gave out. He sat against a tree and peered through the undergrowth back to the river. A flashlight bounced along the bank. McKinnon ducked behind the carcass, peering out from over her front shoulder. Senior had stopped where McKinnon had gutted the doe. The light panned across the river but diffused through the snow.

"You out there, boy?" Senior yelled. McKinnon didn't answer. There was no way Senior could prove he'd been on his property. Then McKinnon remembered the heart. Did he throw it in the river with the rest of the organs? He couldn't remember. Either way, Senior was standing in blood and McKinnon was not convinced enough snow had fallen to cover it.

It snowed nonstop for three days after McKinnon hung the doe inside the shed. The county had all but shut down, only plowing the state highways and salting the roads closest to Caro and the other towns. His mother tasked him with sectioning off an area in the shed to keep the freezer refugees safe from critters and out from under the swinging carcass. He chipped away at the chore during the blizzard. He offered to shovel a walkway for his mother from the front door to the Escort but she refused.

"It doesn't make sense to shovel anything until the last flake lands," she told him. "Besides, we can't get down the drive." McKinnon thought about telling his mother the story of the hunt, how he'd been able to tag a doe he worked twice as hard to get and was rewarded with enough meat to last them a while. He didn't, though; he didn't want her to get angry with him or, worse, to worry about what might have happened had her son got caught. The neighbors, these men with voices louder than the law, wouldn't lose any sleep over the poor McKinnons in the swamp. It was best to lie and tell her he'd downed the doe with a shot that would have even impressed his father. She'd like that.

It stopped snowing early on the fourth day. Sandra woke up just before sunrise and turned on the local news. The storm had dumped close to two feet across the entire Thumb region, the hardest hit area in Michigan. It had come close to breaking a single snowfall record, even. She kicked her feet up on the couch her husband had once claimed for himself and listened as the automatic drip on the coffee maker kicked on. Levon was always around before noon to plow her out. She wasn't in any hurry. She could enjoy her morning.

McKinnon hadn't slept well since returning home. He stayed in bed thinking, still reeling from the hunt and beginning to feel impressed by himself. Eventually he'd tell his mother, years from now. She'd bring up hunting in conversation, something about him having to track a deer farther than he should have, and he'd tell her of the time he pulled a fast one on Rid Sr. and the rest of the uptight neighbors. Probably after Senior was in the ground and the Sterlings had all moved or gone bankrupt or died, whatever happened to folks after they've spent their lives taking and taking and taking. That would be a fun time, McKinnon thought, he and his old mother enjoying the life they'd won, happy to be the last ones standing. He got up just after ten, later than normal, but the doe wasn't going anywhere. His mother was reading on the couch and McKinnon surfed the few TV channels they had.

At two in the afternoon, Levon still had not come to plow the drive.

"He probably had to spend all day plowing himself out," Sandra said across the table as she dished out a bowl of potato soup.

"Probably," McKinnon said.

"Do you need help processing that doe?" she said.

"No, I know how," he said. "I watched Dad a hundred times." He folded his spoon through the thin soup looking for a large chunk of potato.

By noon the next day, Levon still hadn't come and now the snow had an icy crust over it. A chunk cut McKinnon's boot as he pushed through to the shed. The only thing McKinnon knew for sure about processing deer was that his dad let them hang a few days, aging it a little to keep the meat from getting tough. He didn't think the difference between days three and five would matter in the cold, but the edges of exposed muscle had turned black and inedible. Gutting was one thing, a bulk evacuation of organs. Processing, though, required anatomical knowledge of muscle groups, where to cut, how deep, and the intimacy and finesse to not waste any more than he already had. He'd hung the doe from the ceiling with ratchet straps, her front legs crossed behind her head, hooks cut through the tendons at the joints. She swung and spun as McKinnon tried to get a handle of her. Her back hooves scratched across the floor, dancing away from the blade. Gripping her ribs, he tried slicing through the fur at her shoulders but slipped on the frozen blood below her. He fell into the small stack of frozen roasts from his dad's last deer, the knife skittering behind a bag of fertilizer.

The fall knocked the wind from him, and he huddled by the meat, coughing, gasping for a fresh breath in the stale, ammonia air. For all the deer that came before and every sure shot taken to bag them, McKinnon realized that the killing had only been the first step, the easiest, the quickest. The Seniors of the world couldn't stop that from happening, but now McKinnon knew that stopping people from taking any deer they needed wasn't their plan. It was in the slow steps that came after the kill, in the planning for life, the days spent working toward the next, where the real violence happened. The doe towered over McKinnon, the cavity of where her life used to be a gaping mouth laughing at him with ribs like broken, jagged teeth. He found the knife but was not sure where to start or where to go once he did.

Getting Out

Stacey was my PO this time around. She had a small office in a county annex building on Saginaw's east side. Unlike my last PO, Stacey was newer to the job, which was great for guys like me; it meant that she still believed in the work and hadn't been ground down by, well, guys like me. Stacey, in so many words, gave a shit, and that was a good place to start. She even ended every check-in by telling me to "stay successful." I had been out for only four months then but was starting to get the feel for how my life was gonna play out for the next thirty-two: keep working, keep sober, keep my head down. I walked into this last meeting, though, and Stacey didn't have that "stay successful" vibe. She was nose-deep in my file.

"Morning," I said, "that coffee smells good." She motioned for me to sit down.

"Have a seat, Calvin," she said. She didn't look up. "Still at Kroger?"

"Stocking shelves three nights a week," I said. "Going on three months." Most of my coworkers were high school kids and were good for ditching shifts; I was able to pick up three mornings and filled the week working doubles. A landscape crew was unloading one of those zero-turn mowers outside Stacey's window. Used to be that the state or county had inmates do it cheap. I'd done it myself and tried to get on with a new operation out in Caro the first time I was out. That was in the middle of the recession and there were too many folks looking for work who didn't have criminal backgrounds. I didn't stand a chance. Of course, all my file said was I was unemployed at the time of my most recent arrest and now I was barely employed.

"But still no apartment of your own?" She must've really found my file interesting because she hadn't once looked up to me, just kept turning reports over.

"What's with the rapid-fire questions?" I asked.

"Calvin, we're together for three years," she said. "In a perfect world, you find a permanent place to live and a job that can pay for it. Then you keep that job for the duration of your parole. In the real world, you might get fired in, say, a year. You can't pay rent and you have to move. When that happens, I can help, but only if you have a track record of checking off all these little boxes in your file as early as possible. You don't have enough credit."

"Three nights a week on minimum wage doesn't leave me much." I couch surfed for the first month I was out, and now I was trying to make it work at a weekly motel off Michigan Highway 13. Every time I filled out an apartment application, I stopped when it asked, *Have you ever been convicted of a felony?* How was I supposed to make anything more of what I had? The state gave me what they legally determined was enough freedom, but it wasn't enough to grow any kind of new life.

"It's hard finding more work when bosses ask if I got a car," I added.

"You don't have a car?" Stacey paged through my file and jotted down a note.

"Not exactly," I said. "My ex-wife has it. Wouldn't matter much if I had it; I'm not allowed to drive it." One of the landscapers, in a bright green shirt and face mask, glided past the window with a Weedwacker.

"That's not true," Stacey said. She flipped all the way back to the beginning of my file, when I was just Baby Con Cal. "You lost your license on your first arrest because you refused a BAC test then didn't show up for your hearing." She flipped back to the current paper version of me. "You've set up a repayment schedule with Saginaw County; go to the Secretary of State office and get a probationary license. You can drive if it's for work, parole obligations, or emergencies. I mean that, Calvin. If you're caught driving for anything else, with your record, the state of Michigan will send you right back in."

"But I still gotta get my car from my ex," I said.

"That's between you and her," Stacey said. She closed my file and that was that.

Outside at the bus stop I found a bright yellow flyer taped to the glass: *Roommate Needed: All Utilities Included*. It was one of those handmade flyers with the bottom cut into little tearaway phone numbers. Paying weekly at the motel wasn't exactly cost-effective, and with only a hot plate, I wound up ordering takeout a lot. Stacey had mentioned the perfect world and the real world. Maybe being somebody's roomie was a step along that path. Nobody had taken a slip, which meant there was a good chance nobody had called. I took the whole flyer and stuffed it in my back pocket.

I had the rest of the morning off and got out to the Secretary of State. The printer buzzed and the woman behind the counter handed me a form. She pointed at the top of the paper—"Standard Fee: $125"—then to the ATM in the corner. I plugged the amount in, and it spit out a solid chunk of what I'd earned from my extra shifts.

That night at work, I called Kate, my ex, from the pay phone bolted to the storefront. She answered my unknown number with, "Waters-Welch residence," both our last names. She wasn't surprised to hear from me, even asked how I was doing. I told her the good news but didn't know whether to frame getting my license as a celebration or as a favor to her to get the heap out of her driveway.

"I can't just give you the car, Cal," she said.

"But it's mine," I said. "I need it."

"So do I," she said. "The clinic doesn't close just because I'm not there to open the doors." When we were still together, Kate had been chipping away at a business associate's degree. A year into my sentence, she got a job running the office of a veterinary clinic.

"Slip the puppies and kitties some kids' Tylenol and they can sleep the day away," I said.

Kate scoffed.

"That was a joke," I said.

I heard nothing. I could picture her on the other end, formulating how to balance however she'd lived the last three years on her own with me dropping in after a less-than-stellar five years of marriage.

"I'm sorry, Kate," I said.

"It's not an apology issue," she said. "It's a practical one. Let's talk about this later. I'll call you." I tried to tell her this wasn't a cellphone but the line died.

I patted my pockets looking for my cigarettes but realized I must have left the pack in my coat in the break room. I felt the crumpled flyer and pulled it out, flattening it out on the side of the pay phone. I only had two shifts scheduled the coming week. If I had to wait on more money coming in, at least I could slow the bleeding.

I dialed and a man on the other end said he'd meet me at the unit the next evening at seven.

The complex was a quarter mile off the 54 bus line and sat along a tree line behind Rite Aid. It was one of those Bavarian-looking places with the thick, wooden crossbeams over white stucco, inspired by the German immigrants who had flooded mid-Michigan generations ago. It rose three stories from the middle of a dirt parking lot. The spring had been nothing but rain and the lot had flooded until it looked like a wide moat circling a German castle. A man on the third floor sat in a camp chair with his feet up on the balcony railing.

"You Cal?" he called. I said I was and gave a thumbs up. "I'm Mike. C'mon in." I walked into the cleanest, coldest apartment I'd ever been in. Two window units on high, in April! No clutter and everything smelled like lemon and vinegar. A couch sat in the middle of the living room facing the sliding glass balcony door. A small TV stood on an end table in the near corner next to a portable coat rack filled with button ups and slacks. A sliver of counter space divided the living room from an efficiency kitchen. Pretty plain, unassuming, but lined along the back wall were hundreds of boxes of World's Finest chocolate bars. Those cheap ones you get at the bank for a buck, with a Pizza Hut coupon on the wrapper. There must've been close to two thousand chocolate bars stacked in there.

"Nickel tour," Mike said. He had come in from the balcony and was flipping a bottle cap between his knuckles like a magician. He was a small guy, taller than some, shorter than most, kinda soft in the middle, with wispy, light blond hair that sat on his forehead like a tuft of dry hay. He reminded me of this guy at Saginaw Correctional, Scott something-or-other, except this guy, Mike, didn't look like he was gonna kill me for something like sitting in his spot at lunch. He was unassuming like the apartment except for the perfect seams in his clothes, like he was dressed in origami.

"Bedroom's through the door there on the left," he said. "Bathroom's on the right. You can have the bedroom. I've been sleeping on this couch here for so long that I think my body would shut down if I used a bed anymore. There's some linens in the closet. Rent's due on the last day of the month."

I pointed to the wall of boxes.

"Product," he said. He mimed straightening a necktie. "I'm a salesman. When you're all settled in, come out to my office. I've got an opportunity I know will interest you." He flipped the bottlecap like a coin and caught it as he turned back to the balcony.

The bedroom was clean and empty like the rest of the apartment but thankfully warmer. A twin bed sat in one corner below an open window, and a small school desk sat in the other. A poster of the Eiffel Tower hung above the desk and someone had written JUNE at the top so it looked like it was balancing on the tip of the tower. The closet had a couple pink sheets, a pillow, and a bright purple comforter. I threw my bag on the desk and made the bed. I had treated myself to some new clothes from Goodwill to celebrate my newfound, curtailed freedom. Two gray denim pants and a navy-blue Columbia jacket, the kind that zipped all the way to my chin. When I tried it on, I looked like a banker or a college student on his way to get Starbucks. That is, if nobody looked at my shoes.

When I went outside, Mike handed me a folded camp chair.

"Have a seat, Cal," he said. The balcony fit the two of us snugly. A Burger King bag and two empty Bud Light bombers were below his chair, and he had a third bottle set on the clipboard across his lap. My tongue tensed as it remembered the chill of a night's first beer. Then I thought of Stacey's warning, the piss test I'd woken up early that day to drop, and jail. Mike handed me a burger.

"I knew who I was asking to room with when I posted those flyers," he said. "A salesman doesn't just know the product; he knows the buyer. Did you find the one outside the probation/parole office or the piss test lab?"

"Probation and parole," I said. I bit into the burger, pulled the tomato out, and set it on the wrapper.

"Need to save money, eh?" he asked. "Want to make more?"

"What's the catch?" I asked.

"Just do as I say and I'll pay you a hundred a week or take it off rent. Your choice." He tapped the clipboard resting in his lap. "I clear four hundred bucks a week."

"Pay me one-fifty and we have a deal." He twisted the cap off his beer and balanced it on his thumb like a coin.

"Watch this," he said. He flipped the cap and caught it midair by its edge. With a jerk of his wrist, he snapped his finger and the cap spun out toward the tree line. It spiraled through the leaves like a flying saucer and disappeared into the dark. He chuckled to himself and drank. "My dad taught me that," he said. "Here it is: I know what I'm seeing because I've seen it before. Been there myself. I was in. Now I'm out. Going on seven years of what the state calls 'free.' I got tired of part-timing it and tired of managers with their finger over the employment-at-will button. I know you need this, and I know that I didn't have help when I was where you are."

I wasn't on the lease, so I could bail if Mike really was a nut. If he wasn't, though, maybe I could bank enough to not need my car.

"Sold for a hundred a week," I said.

"Great. We start tomorrow at nine."

———

"Wakey, wakey, Cal," Mike called. He rapped his knuckles on my door. I had fallen asleep in my clothes and woke feeling like I was wearing wet leaves. Kate had gotten most of my stuff when I'd gone down. Not that there was much to be had. We'd lived in a double-wide up in the Thumb, just outside Caro. She sold it. Had a joint checking account she'd mostly emptied by the time I got out. Though she did leave me a few hundred dollars I used to get myself started at the motel. All I had were the clothes Saginaw County gave back to me, black jeans and a Lynyrd Skynyrd T-shirt, and the new Goodwill clothes.

I threw on the new pants and jacket and went out. Mike had four boxes stacked in his arms and he had me grab four more. There were so many that half the wall looked like it was made up of them, stacked like castle bricks. I stumbled down the stairs behind Mike, trying my best not to drop anything while keeping up with the guy as he all but ran toward his car, sidestepping puddles and Styrofoam cups along the way.

"Stack them in the back," he said, "carefully so they don't tip over. Then go up and grab four more." The car was freezing too, the AC crackling through the vents. He handed me a travel coffee mug when I climbed in the front. "Black with sugar."

It was warm for a Michigan April. Days were keeping up near seventy and an early thaw had washed over everything. The ground was letting everything run from it and long ruts of mud streaked over the sidewalks to the gutters. It was like the whole earth had drunk too much failure and was trying to not swallow any more. We drove along a boarded-up strip of buildings, a closed-down body shop, a soup kitchen that was only open on Sundays. The city had been terminal for decades and the recession had pushed it to the breaking point. In the three years that I'd been gone, a lot of the joints I'd called home had died. Buford's Billiards, The Plaid Palace, even the corner party store that sold loosie cigarettes was all plywood and graffiti. The only things that plugged along were dollar stores, fast food, and gas stations.

I didn't believe Mike had just chocolate bars in those boxes. He wasn't the only one who knew what he saw because he'd seen it before. I had begun to spend more and more time in Saginaw in the months before I'd been picked up for selling shit from the trunk of my Lumina. Had me a job at the GM foundry and was trying for my UAW card, knowing full well I'd be laid off before my ninety days. Union lifers didn't want to share and, in many ways, treated guys like me, nobodies, just like management treated us: replaceable. I had come out after a shift one night to find a couple cops had jimmied open my trunk and were bagging up everything they found: a couple car stereos, some iPads, lengths of copper pipes and wiring. Security camera had caught me selling the night before, what a dummy move. Three years later I was shotgun, pushing, surrounded by empty buildings, and not blaming Mike one damn bit.

We headed west into the township, an area crammed with subdivisions and churches. Mike pulled into a nondenominational parking lot and grabbed his clipboard and folder from the glove compartment.

"Hand me two boxes," he said. "Stay here and keep the AC going." Twenty minutes later, he was back, boxes gone. We repeated this at half a dozen churches, most taking both boxes except for the Methodists who didn't take any. Mike scratched a note next to it on the clipboard and said they'd be good for three, at least, the next time around. By noon, we were closer to the city limits, stopping at the large assisted-living complexes that filled the area. Each stop taking longer than the last.

"So," I finally asked, "how much you getting for this stuff?"

"A dollar per."

"That's it?"

"That's what the boxes say."

"Seems like a deal to me," I said.

"You'd think," he said, "but the seniors still try haggling me down to seventy-five cents. They aren't even supposed to have this stuff, so I gotta keep firm with them. I don't want to waste my time."

Just after three, Mike pulled off in front of an elementary school. Kids filed into rows of buses, and I thought selling to Jesus freaks and old timers was one thing, but this was too much.

Before I could protest, he got out of the car and leaned on the hood. I started sweating and the AC froze to me. I sank into the passenger's seat and waited. The thought of a judge finding out that I was caught selling candy and God knows what else to children made me itch. Then Mike stood up as a girl in a unicorn hoodie and a purple backpack ran out to him. She had tight brown braids with tiny purple bows. He picked her up in a hug and spun her around so she could stand on the hood of the car, making her slightly taller than Mike. They said a few words and he pointed at me. The girl stared me down through the windshield.

"Cal," Mike said, "Janie rides shotgun. Jump in back. Honey, this is Cal, my roommate." I held the door for her before climbing to the middle of the backseat.

"Can you work?" she said. She was clutching a stack of books to her chest.

"Yes, boss," I said. I saluted her. We pulled in among the rows of buses and headed back out to the township. Everything was brown and water-logged, even on this side of the river.

"I think we should hit the apartment complexes by the college," Mike said.

"There won't be many people around," Janie said.

"Why not?" I asked.

"Because it's Friday, duh."

"Ah, right you are," Mike said. "What about the subdivisions out west?"

"I can work with that," Janie said.

The houses in the subdivision were as big as the entire complex Mike and I were staying in. He parked the car at the bend of a cul-de-sac.

"Remember the script?" he asked her. This big smile grew across her face, complete with bright purple braces. She pushed the glasses up off her nose and cleared her throat. She looked like she was pretending to be a news anchor.

"Hello, my name is Janie Rebutte and I'm selling candy for a school fundraiser." She sounded like she could train the Girl Scouts.

"And if they say no?"

"Keep at it. Tell them how it will help me."

"And?"

"And . . ." She trailed off, trying to remember. She grabbed her braids and looked to me as if I knew the answer.

"You tell them how proud you are to be earning your own way," he said.

"Right!" Janie said, and her smile returned. "I want to earn it myself." She jumped out and tapped on my window pointing to the boxes. "Don't forget, you gotta work," she said. I grabbed one and slid it through the window. She ran up a brick path to one of the houses and rang the bell. A lady with a phone wedged between her shoulder and ear answered. Janie opened the box and after a moment, the lady hung up the phone, pulled some cash from her pocket, and took a few bars. Janie did a quick bounce where she stood before turning to run back down the path and up the one at the next house.

Mike idled the car, letting it creep along behind the girl as she made her way from door to door.

"She's really got a knack for this," I said. It floored me how bouncy Janie was. The girl had just spent all day in school and was now helping her dad push through his supply as if it were the one thing she looked forward to all day.

"People in the suburbs love this stuff," Mike said. He gave a thumbs-up out the window to Janie when she and a man in a camo apron that said *The Buck (and Doe) Stops Here* waved. "Especially him. He's probably bought two boxes himself. It's addicting."

I watched from the back seat and by the tenth house, Janie returned with an empty box and fifty dollars in singles and fives.

"Dad," she said, "that last man gave me ten dollars and told me to keep the change!" She tapped on my window, and I slid out another full box.

"That's great, honey," he said. "Keep at it." She ran back up the sidewalk and we followed. We weaved through the subdivision until it started getting dark and Mike called Janie to get in.

"Let's get some chow," Mike said. He pulled out of the subdivision and Janie handed the clipboard back to me. The sheet was a grid with today's date and the names of the places we'd hit.

"Put tallies by the dollar amounts," she said. She counted the ones first then moved up the denominations. She had cleaned house. There were only a few loose bars sitting next to me on the bench. I was finishing adding the tallies when the car began to shudder. Then, a loud clanging came from under the car.

"Hold on," Mike said. The car lurched onto the shoulder, and we were almost sideways as we hit the dirt. Mike pressed one arm across Janie while trying to straighten us out with the other but in a flash, the nose tipped into the ditch.

———

We jammed onto the wrecker's bench seat. Janie sat in Mike's lap, her legs curled against the dash. I sat in the middle with my hands under my thighs and my knees tucked together. I had to lean into Mike so the driver could shift gears.

"Can we still get dinner?" Janie asked. "I can pay for my own."

"Might have to be mac and cheese, honey," Mike said. He was calculating costs on his clipboard: the price of repairs, the shrinkage of his selling radius from driving distance to walking, rent and utilities. Heaven forbid he buy a beer or food. He had been smooth the night before, and I was impressed with the bookkeeping, clearing enough to get by but not enough to get clear.

"My treat," I said. "A thank you for letting me tag along."

There was a Mickey D's up the road from the garage and we ate our burgers in the play area while Janie crouched her way through the yellow and green plastic tubes. Mike called his ex-wife and told her the news.

"Do you have more buyers lined up?" I asked.

"Churches buy about twice a month," Mike said. "I can't rely on them until next week and nobody is keen to buy from a middle-aged man going door to door."

"Can you raise prices?"

"The company won't allow it."

"What do you mean, 'the company?'" I asked. He had his burger to his lips and cocked an eyebrow. "Those are just plain chocolate bars, aren't they?"

"Some have nuts in them," Mike said.

"That's it?"

"They're just chocolate, man. That's it." He shook his head and went back to eating his dinner. Before my last arrest, I knew the codes pushers used around mid-Michigan. Back home in Caro, *sugar beets* meant cocaine, and nobody looked sideways if somebody had a *prescription*. *Candy* wasn't exactly subtle, but I'd heard it used before. I called the iPads in the Lumina's trunk *spark plugs*. It wasn't that I cared if Mike was still a criminal; I assumed that he was doing the best he could with what the world dealt him. He said himself that selling was all he could find, and if his PO was anything like my first, he didn't get much help in finding legitimate employment. I called it the criminal carousel: The state just kept us spinning.

"What about the AC?"

"Nobody wants to buy melted chocolate." I saw him crunching the numbers in his head. "Janie's mom signed her up for a French course six months ago," he said. "A college kid tutors her. Janie, how are your French lessons going?"

She popped her head out of a tube and yelled, "Jam apple Janie!" then disappeared again. He bit into his burger, and a gob of ketchup pooled in the corner of his mouth.

"See? She's almost got it. Been stuck at almost getting it for a while now, so this tutor convinced her mother that the best way to perfect French is to go to France." He ate and I watched Janie go down the slide then climb back up the way she came. She couldn't have been any older than eleven. I thought about that poster hanging in my bedroom, how JUNE teetering at the top of the Eiffel Tower was Mike's goal, and how it was six weeks away. I may not have been able to leave the county, but I knew enough that cardboard boxes with a few crumbled singles in them weren't going to cut it.

"Isn't her mom helping?"

"Told me she'd pay for expenses in France just so long as I got Janie there. That's fair," he said. "Rent went up but I got it calculated that with your help, we can do it."

Janie ran up to the table and popped a chicken nugget into her mouth before she disappeared again. "And her?" I asked.

"Her mother wasn't too keen on me taking her every afternoon during the week. I told her it would teach Janie responsibility and that my dad had me selling Boy Scout popcorn by the time I was nine. She eventually agreed with the condition that I gave up some weekend visits. Give and take, you know? Her mother's always been a straight shooter."

When Janie's mother came to get her, she hugged Mike and asked if anyone was hurt. They sat down inside the restaurant's main dining room to talk. She sipped from his pop and had I not known it, I'd have sworn they were happily married. I wondered if Kate and I could be like them one day. Janie took Mike's spot at the table.

"You looking forward to your trip?" I asked. "See the Eiffel Tower and all that?" I wolfed down a handful of fries.

"Can you keep a secret?" She dipped a nugget in ketchup. I said I could. "I don't think I'm going to France anymore. I googled plane tickets. Math's my favorite subject. I know my dad can't afford it."

"That's why he hired me," I said. "More sellers to raise more money."

"But he has to pay you so what's the point?" We both stared through the glass to her parents. Mike was pointing at the clipboard. She was pointing at her watch. "I don't want to make them sad," Janie said. Her parents knocked on the glass and waved Janie to come inside. She kissed Mike on the cheek and walked out holding her mother's hand, sipping Hi-C.

In bed that night, I stared at the poster of the Eifel Tower and pictured Mike caught at the top of it, balancing chocolate bars in one hand, his family in the other, and his clipboard between his teeth. The guy talked like someone who had it all under control, or at least more so than me. He talked through the rapid-fire agreement, the done-onto-the-next-one selling, all while not knowing that the one person he was trying to help was losing faith in him.

———

The next morning was Saturday. Mike was curled up on the couch with his head buried in the back cushion. I put on clean clothes, took the 54 bus, connected with the 1 bus, then settled in as I made my way west through the city. Kate owned a small house past the township, beyond the big houses where Janie and Mike sold. I knew she made the schedule at the vet clinic, one of the perks of being a manager, and I hoped she'd given herself the weekend off. Her house was a mile and a half north of the last bus stop, and sitting out front was my green Lumina. There was no guarantee that she was going to let me have it. She used to say the only two things that can make a person mean are time and other people. With me, she'd had both.

There was a spring wreath hanging on her front door filled with fake flowers and little foam birds. I rang the new video doorbell thing in the middle of it and waited.

Oh my God, Cal? the doorbell said. I leaned into the black dot of the camera and put on my cheesy grin.

"Honey, I'm home," I said. Kate came to the door in one of my old Pink Floyd T-shirts. "Nice shirt."

"Call it alimony," Kate said. I was about to say something, but she cut me off. "That's a joke." She closed the door behind her, and I backed off her porch to the steps leading up to it. "If you're here about the car, I told you I need it."

"What about your car?"

"Cal, that Escort was already fifteen years old by the time we got married. I was lucky to get $1,200 for it. You don't think the world just stopped when you went to prison, do you?"

"No," I said. Of course I didn't believe that.

I told her about Mike and Janie, about the chocolate bars and France, about the busted car and splitting a one-bedroom apartment. Kate sat down on the steps as I kept going. I told her that these were people trying to turn their getting by into something more, and while I was telling her this, I found that my chest hurt and my eyes burned.

"They sound like good people, Cal," she said. "But I still need the car. I work and have some doctor appointments. I have a life." I tried to think about the smooth confidence Mike used on me and what he'd said about knowing who he was selling to. Kate and I had a dance routine when we fought, a real simple two-step where I said one thing and she said the opposite. Then we'd spin around and not get anywhere.

"Are you willing to make a deal?" I asked. That was not my usual move, and she was right, the world didn't stop when I went away, and the people didn't either. "I will drive you wherever you need to go if you let me have the car during the day."

"I work five days a week," she said.

"So do I."

"I'm up early."

"So am I."

She dropped her head forward, almost to her knees, and let out a long groan.

"One week," she said, lifting her head. "We'll try it out for one week. If I'm late to anything, I'm ditching you at the closest bus stop."

"Deal," I said.

The driver's seat was warm from the sun and the car smelled like Kate's shampoo, rosemary and mint. She leaned into the window.

"When did you become the happy helper type?" she asked.

"Someone once told me the only things that can change a person are time and other people."

"Sounds like a smart person," she said.

Mike was out on the balcony when I got home.

"Your chariot awaits," I yelled. I spread my arms out over the Lumina. He lifted his beer toward me and snapped a bottle cap. It bounced off the roof of the car.

———

On Monday I dropped Kate off early at work. She'd been kind enough to take a box of chocolate for the front counter. I told her I'd be back before two to get her to an appointment and that Mike would be with me.

The morning was brutal. Only half a box sold to the college kids at Saginaw Valley and the owner of a barbershop almost shoved me out of his store when I refused to trade him a box for a buzzcut. We had coffees for lunch. I fished a dollar out of my wallet and traded it for a crispy rice chocolate bar.

"Can't have many more days like this so close to the deadline," Mike said. He was tallying on his clipboard. I broke a chunk of chocolate in my mouth and pulled into the west side Kroger. I fished my employee vest from under the seat and two boxes from the back.

"Stay here," I said. "Keep the AC going." It wasn't my store, but they all looked the same: same workers, same aisle numbers. Same door past the bathrooms where employees took their breaks. Inside, half a dozen people were eating sandwiches and salads from the deli.

"My son's puppy has cancer and I'm trying to raise money for the vet bills," I said.

Back at the car, I handed one hundred dollars in tens and twenties to Mike.

"We've got an appointment to keep," I said.

———

That afternoon, Janie, Mike, and I were outside the Saginaw Township Health Annex where we'd dropped Kate off. I was antsy because we'd only sold two more boxes that day. Janie wasn't running up to houses, and too many times the homeowners slammed the door in her face before she'd had the chance to show them the goods. She was up front next to me. I put another dollar in the box and handed her a caramel bar. She bit one corner and squeezed the caramel out. Kate came out and sat in back with Mike. They shook hands and Kate leaned forward.

"And you must be Janie," she said. "I hear you're quite the little saleswoman."

"You wanna buy one?" Janie said. She held the box open toward Kate.

"I probably shouldn't," she said. "Too many refined sugars. But here." She fished in her purse and pulled out some money. "Cal gave me a box for my job, and this is what I made this morning." There were about fifteen dollars in a paper clip. I winked at Kate through the rearview.

"Is that what the doctor said?" I asked. "You okay?"

"I'm perfectly fine," Kate said.

"A perfectly fine person doesn't have so many doctor appointments," I said.

"In vitro," Mike said. Kate put her hand over her eyes, her thumb and middle finger stretching the edges of her eyes. We had fought over kids our entire marriage. It was our favorite two-step. I wanted them. She didn't.

"I don't mean to pry," Mike said. "Congratulations."

"How did you know?" Kate said.

"Cal told me the schedule," he said. "And I know what I'm seeing because I've seen it before. Same schedule, same clinic, even the same door me and my ex walked through." He pulled himself forward and kissed Janie on the top of her head. "Worth everything," he said.

Kate and I saw each in the rearview. I wanted to be angry and to feel betrayed. But all I felt was left behind.

We said our goodbyes in Kate's driveway, and she told me she was taking the next couple days off and to not worry about driving her anywhere. It felt like a consolation, like ginger ale for a stomachache when what I needed was real medicine.

"Good luck, Janie," Kate said. "If your father worked so hard to have you, I know he'll work harder to help you succeed."

We dropped Janie off at a split-level north of the city. Her mother waved to us from the front porch. I flashed the high beams. Mike was all smiles.

"You two seem married," I said. "What happened?" Mike and I were on the same road it seemed, but he was navigating it with way more skill than me.

"Prison happened," Mike said. "She couldn't tie herself to that part of me and she definitely couldn't tie Janie to it. I can't blame her for that."

"Couldn't you try again?"

"This isn't make believe, Cal. We make deals and decisions that either bring us closer to others or tear us apart."

———

It rained all the way into June, as if the early thaw and wet spring weren't enough. Everything was drowning and smelled like stale motor oil. Every morning, I left early to take Kate to work. Then we all carpooled home. On Mondays, Mike and I took Kate to and from her appointments. Each time he'd ask her about her progress. Each time I'd get a little happier for her. We raised about nine hundred dollars for Janie, and she was only two weeks from flying out. I harbored hopes that we could pull it off for her. I was asleep after five days of doubles when Mike poked my side, waking me up.

"Let's go, man," he said, "we got someplace to be." His eyes were swollen, and he had a half empty bottle of Burnett's in one hand and an entire case of Coors Light in the other. He stood, rocking back and forth, and pulled long from the plastic bottle. I started to remind him that I couldn't drive for fun, but he was already gone.

Out in the parking lot, he barreled through the puddles. He turned at the driver's door and wedged the Burnett's bottle into the corner of his mouth and his hand into his pocket.

"Whoa, Mike," I called, "you ain't going anywhere like that." I was hopping on one foot, still trying to get my other shoe on. He underhanded the keys at me like a softball pitcher having a bad game. I covered my face as the clanging ring flew toward my head. They fell into a puddle behind me. I slipped my hand into the filthy water and groped around, hoping I didn't rip my hand open on glass.

"Let's go." Again, I tried telling him I couldn't drive but he wasn't having it. "There's a difference between can't and shouldn't, Cal. Now get in."

———

"Take 81 east," Mike said, "out past Caro. Turn off when I tell you." He didn't say anything for a long while after that, just kept that case of beer snug in his lap. I took my time working my way through the east side. Gave extra care at the intersections and made sure not to speed through the easy curves out by the foundry. Mike hit the bottle and cracked the window. The night was warm and I could feel the heat coming up from the road. We got out past the interstate, where Tuscola County started, where there weren't any more streetlights, just farmland, stars, and the heavy buzz of the high-power electric wires that stitched it all together.

"What's the play here, boss?" I said. "We've got selling to do in the morning."

"Take tomorrow off," he said. "Hell, take the whole week off."

"What are you talking about?"

"Ask Janie." He rolled the window down the rest of the way and spit.

"She ain't here," I said. "What happened?"

"She quit French lessons. Her mother said she wasn't taking to it and wanted to quit. So she let her."

"That can't be the end of it," I said. "What about all the money?"

"Of course that's the end of it," Mike said. "This isn't life, Cal, it's business. The cost analysis said we were doomed. So, the higher-ups liquidated." He drank.

"Well can't you—" I started.

"You know, Janie," he interrupted, leaning back to talk to the empty back seat. "My dad signed me up for Little League when I was about your age. The first game of the season, I was in the outfield and I watched my best buddy take a line drive. Smack! Straight to the face. Broke his nose and his cheekbone just like that. After the game, I told my dad I wanted to quit. Know what he said to me?"

"It's just me and you, Mike," I said.

"Nothing," Mike continued. "He beat my ass. It was his way of telling me to keep at it. And I did, made varsity my sophomore year. I made your grandfather proud, goddamn it. And that's close enough to love." He stuck his head out the window and retched. With one hand on the wheel, I leaned over and patted his back before pulling him back in.

"Keep going until you're on the far side of Caro," he said.

Caro was a city only in name, really, and most places were closed for the night. All the traffic lights had switched over to blinking yellows and we passed through without stopping. When Mike told me to pull over, we were up along the chain-link fence of a township cemetery ten miles past the city limits. It was already getting dark, and if any other car had been out on the roads, we'd have seen their headlights coming from miles away.

They don't lock many things up that far out and there was only a fork-latch gate across the entrance path. The smell of dying flowers mixed with the oily earth smell of the rusting fence. Everything was one blurry, muddy shadow. Mike stood at the gate, white-knuckling the beer and half pint, for what seemed like a lifetime, staring past me at the rows and rows of names and dates and buried lives. At the rows of stones and crosses and angels.

"C'mon, man," I said. "Why are we here?"

Mike finished the half pint and wiped the corners of his mouth on his sleeve as he slipped past me. Then, as if something in him had switched on, he started running down the first row of gravestones. He was gone so fast that the only thing I thought was to keep up. So, I ran after him. Every fourth marker or so, he would stop and crouch down real close to the engravings. He'd stay like that for a moment, hugging the beer to his chest, with his face almost pressed against the slab of granite.

"Is that you, Dad?" he said. It looked like he was letting his mind catch up to the rest of him, as if his body remembered some ingrained instinct or habit that walking through the cemetery gate had triggered. He just went, quick like a snap, and his reason for running the rows was a good thirty yards behind him. He was two men running at different speeds. When he caught up with himself, he'd shake his head and mutter to himself, then he'd be off again, curling around the dead Smiths and Parkers, the groundskeeper's shed. I matched him step for step until I started tripping over bouquets of plastic flowers and veteran wreathes. He had gotten about twenty yards away from me and I tried calling out to him but tripped on one of those grave markers that are supposed to lay flush with ground. I hit the soaked ground and got a face full of grass clippings. Mike cut out a short laugh. When I looked up, he was nose to nose with another gravestone.

"Found you," he said.

"Found what?" I asked. I wiped myself off as I walked up to him.

"*Who*," Mike said, "not *what*. These are people, you know."

I crouched down next to him and squinted through the dark at the engraving:

Michael B. Rebutte

1949–2009

Husband—Father

"You died in 2009, buddy?" I asked. "You look good for a dead guy." Mike collapsed in the wet grass next to the headstone. The case of beer fit between his legs like a present and he ripped it open. He pulled out the first bottle and untwisted the cap.

"Watch this, Dad," he said to the stone. He snapped the cap and it quickly disappeared in the night. "Just how you taught me."

I leaned on a gravestone just across the row and wondered if Mike was going to drink that entire case and, if so, how long it would take him. But he didn't drink that first beer. Instead, he tipped the beer out over his dad's grave and let the whole thing pour out onto the already drunk earth. Then he reached for a second beer and did the same thing, a twist, a snap, and a long pour. No sip for himself, not even a whiff, he made sure all of it flowed out onto his dad's head. Then the third. The fourth.

"Was gonna bring Janie to see ya," Mike said. "But she quit on me, Dad. All I got is Cal." He poured another beer and its sweet yeast smell began to waft into the dark. I remembered what Janie told me that day at McDonald's and wondered if this was what she meant by making her dad sad. It wasn't his fault that he was forced to play without a full deck. But it wasn't Janie's fault for not wanting to play a rigged game.

"Mr. Rebutte," I said. I moved over to the opposite side of the head-stone and put my arm around it like I was talking to an old friend. "Your son has been good to me but he ain't telling you the whole story." I kicked an empty bottle. Mike was quiet. "Go on, tell him how much she made."

"R-right," he said. "She had a knack for it. 'Goal-driven' as you used to say, Dad." He grabbed another beer and poured. "No, Pop, she doesn't play baseball. Yes, Pop, you pushed me—That's not what I'm saying.

She can play if she wants to, but I'm not going to make her—Yes, I was good."

I watched the Mikes talk and I saw how a single body could carry with it two lives: one that walks through the day, balancing every deal and decision needed to be made with who will benefit or hurt from them, planning for the countless tomorrows and familiar cycles to come. The second, a life always awake in the way things used to be, sitting in a thousand yesterdays of fast food, jungle gyms, and PO piss tests, dancing to the tune of every needless argument. It went on and on and on and, I swear, I didn't want it to end. I reached into the case for a bottle. I twisted the cap off and balanced the small tab on my thumb before flicking it into the air like a coin.

TOO CLOSE, TOO LOUD

Bright flags hung along the low fence lining the street and someone had covered old campaign yard signs with homemade FOR SALE ads. *All Labor Day Weekend* one said in red, white, and blue. The others had strips of duct tape across them, covering up big ticket items that Delaney Southby-Chuberts had missed out on. She rarely went out the last day of a long weekend, but her poor takes the first two days had forced her to scavenge. Only two trucks lined the side of the dirt driveway leading to a large farmhouse. Out back were two old sheds, but another sign posted in the yard stated that the sale had shrunk to just the contents of the house. Delaney parked close to the front and waved to the two women sitting on the porch swing. One was drinking a lemonade, the other a Coors.

"Morning," Delaney said. The women gave small nods but said nothing to her. Instead, the lemonade woman leaned over and whispered something to the Coors woman as Delaney entered the house. Delaney grabbed a stack of green Post-it notes and a pen from the counter, ready to stake claims on whatever she found. Labor Day was a big deal for her resale website, Delaney's Discounts & Designs. She had it marked in her calendar as the year's last opportunity to scour garage and estate sales across the county before she was forced to make do on shelf-stuffers from Goodwill. She went into the countryside while her half sister, Allison, was still home for the summer and hit smaller sales in town. However, 2019 hadn't turned out as she would have liked. Prices were higher and folks seemed less willing to haggle. Up through the previous year, she could undersell other resale places and sometimes even major websites, but she had needed to raise prices on some of her inventory. Besides a denim jacket and snow pants, the first three sales had yielded a single cordless drill, of which she already had three, and a handmade rocker with arms stained black from years of hand sweat.

Delaney zeroed in on a KitchenAid stand mixer that she could easily make a bill from. She wrote *DDD* on the first sticky note, slapped it on the mixer, and was on her way. Despite the downturn, Delaney enjoyed estate sales. She could walk around the home, see where the walls had rubbed down near the light switches, see the living room set up with a floor lamp tucked either to the right or left of an armchair, walk along the worn carpeting as if she were part of the home. She pretended she was the shadow of the families that used to live there. She made up stories as she hunted, then turned those stories into sales pitches for her website. *Constant companion marked with love* was a good fit for the stained armchair. Or something like that. She wanted her customers to feel like they were buying more than someone else's junk.

The kitchen drawers were empty and a chest freezer already had a pink Post-it with *SANDRA McKINNON* written on it. No matter, Delaney wrote *+$10: DDD* on a note and stuck it next to the pink one. In the den, an old love seat, frayed on the sides where a cat had clawed at it, sat on a brown and orange area rug. No resale value there, Delaney noted. A length of binder twine across the staircase told Delaney that the bedrooms had already sold out. If the mixer really was the only thing to come from the forty-minute drive, then she'd price it at $150, buy up the commemorative JFK plates hanging on the wall, and call the day a marginal win. Turning back into the kitchen, the two women stood by the mixer.

"Nice day," Delaney said.

"Been a good weekend for us," the lemonade woman said.

"You're Delaney," the beer woman said. She was holding both green Post-its.

"I am."

"You run that place north of Caro, the, the, what's its name?" The lemonade woman snapped and twirled her fingers at the side of her head. "Delaney's Dirt-Cheap Doodads."

"Delaney's Discounts & Designs."

"Yeah, that."

"I'm sorry," the beer woman said. "The mixer is already spoken for." She folded the two notes into tiny green strips.

"There wasn't a name on it," Delaney said.

"Must've fallen off," the lemonade woman said. She sipped her drink and the condensation dripped onto her shirt.

"What are they giving you for it?" she asked. "I'll go five higher."

"Look, if it's all the same to you, we'd rather you not take the mixer."

"Why not?"

"We don't like what you do."

"I sell things. Same as you're doing here," Delaney said. The Coors woman folded the note again, handing it to the other woman who tucked it into her back pocket.

"My mother left behind a lot of memories and the people buying are the people she'd want to have her stuff anyway," she said.

"She used that mixer when she baked for her neighbors," the lemonade woman said. "The person who buys it will do the same. It's called *tradition*."

"Something you're too young to appreciate," the beer woman said. "But that's expected from someone who sells to names on a screen."

"I sell to who buys."

"We've got enough of the world coming in," the beer woman said. "We aren't going to help with parts of it going out."

"What do you want for the JFK plates?"

"They're not for sale," both women said.

In the truck heading home, half a tank of gas gone, Delaney calculated how much the trip had cost her. She cursed the women, the way they waved goodbye with their fingers, as if they were casting a spell against her. And what was that *tradition* bullshit? She was a born-and-raised Thumbody, lived and worked it, stayed when so many her age had left. A sales pitch for the KitchenAid came to her as she pulled into her driveway: *A life's worth of confectionary comfort.* That was a great one, wasted because of those women.

Delaney was in the third year of a land contract for a two-bedroom house wedged on the back of a half acre of rezoned farmland. It had been a thirtieth birthday gift to herself, supplemented by a small slice of a life insurance policy left by Al Southby, her adoptive father. The house wasn't a lot but the large pole barn on the other side of the property had been a major selling point for her. She had envisioned opening the two-car garage door during the summer to make an open-air pop-up shop to supplement her online sales. Delaney had dickered down cost when a wind energy survey crew came to approve the erection of a turbine. That meant months of building culverts, access roads, foundations, the turbine itself. More crews, more trucks, cranes, noise upon noise, and something called "shadow flicker." None of this bothered Delaney, in fact, but the farmer selling to her didn't need to know that. As she saw it, anything to lower overhead was a win.

She laid on some of the conspiracies she'd heard from folks around town: the flicker might turn her blind; the Deep State used them as surveillance; their hum kept the countryside awake. Truth be told, she loved watching from her back porch as the crews worked, and when the first semi came, hauling the base of the tower, she felt as if she were sitting front row to the future. Taller and wider than the semi that hauled it, decked out in flashing warning lights, the base of the tower looked like a giant steel worm about to devour the truck. The driver inched onto the access road that only weeks before had been a rusted culvert.

Then the turbine blades came, stretching fifty yards from the access road back to the previous intersection. Spotters blocked off traffic, walking the length of the oversize load trailer, as the driver inched into a wide turn. Like magic, the hydraulic rear of the trailer maneuvered itself along the turn, swinging the tip of the blade over Delaney's mailbox. Five months later, the turbine was up and running, 150 yards back from the property. On clear days, the sun reflected off the nacelle and shadows from the blades ran across the yard and into the road. Delaney took photos and tried selling prints on her site. The profile of the turbine against the pink-red-orange sunrise. A blade shadow stretched over a green combine as it harvested wheat, chaff swirling on the wind. Like her other photos and collages, hardly any sold.

Delaney lugged the stained rocker and shelf-stuffers through the garage door. A makeshift wall of accent room dividers and workbenches divided the space in two. Wood furniture, a gun safe, and an array of gardening supplies filled one side of the barn. The office computer and another safe for Delaney's camera equipment sat in the front, and a stretch of canvas lined the wall, covering boxes of old photographs she and Allison had found at sales. The other side of the barn acted as Allison's workshop during the summer. A row of push mowers sat up front with Sharpied price tags zip-tied to the handles. Priced power tools hung on a pegboard spanning the wall. Jacked up in the back was the sisters' big project for the last eighteen months, a 1976 Pontiac Grand Prix 455-4 that Delaney had found two towns over, neglected under an old camo tarp. Allison was at the driver's side wheel well, squatting as she positioned the tire into place.

"Sold a mower and a set of wrenches today," she said. "Sixty bucks, total." She flipped on an air compressor and its rattle filled the space.

The previous summer, the barn always had plenty of room. Merchandise went out daily by mail and there were always people shopping in person. Now, it was cramped, despite Delaney moving all the collectibles and clothing into the house. Delaney brought up her spreadsheets and logged the day's purchases, thirty dollars. That weekend marked a new month, with August being the seventh month where sales failed to match the previous. Delaney couldn't deny it anymore; after three years of resale boom, she was in her own little recession.

That night, Delaney couldn't fall asleep. She had lost out on deals before, been late to sales, and completely blew it the one time she'd tried her hand at an auction. But those women with the KitchenAid had gotten to her and made every inch of her prickle with heat. Her pillow was soggy with sweat. People didn't seem to want to understand she was nothing more than a worker. Being hand-to-mouth was practically her DNA with time and money spiraling into the double helix. She couldn't sleep because those sisters had wasted her time and because of that, her money. She could hear their voices, as if they were standing over her bed, droning and droning and droning until she realized what she was hearing was the turbine blades spinning from the field. She buried her head under her pillow, clenching her teeth until she heard nothing but the pumping of blood in her temples, and then nothing at all.

————

Delaney woke to a power drill whirring in the living room. Allison had her hair tied back by a red handkerchief, sleeves rolled, and was fastening together two lengths of two-by-four.

"You make out at any sales?" Delaney said over the drill. Allison held a screw in the corner of her mouth and kept her eyes on her work.

"Free lumber," Allison said. She lipped the screw from one corner of her mouth to the other before grabbing it out and driving it into the wood. Allison had removed piles of merchandise—mostly tops and pants Delaney had already uploaded to the site—to make space in the corner of the living room. "Check this out." She tucked the drill under her arm and twisted the vertical two-by-four, which allowed her to lift and secure the horizontal board backward and up. "You can put another board here now for more space," she said. She twisted again and the beam slid back down.

"That'll help," Delaney said. "But any new merch?" She sidestepped the pile into the kitchen where fresh coffee waited for her.

"No," Allison called. "We didn't have the room until now." The drill whirred some more as she put the finishing touches onto the rack.

Outside the kitchen window, Delaney saw a green pickup truck rumble into the driveway. Across the side read *Greatest of All Time Landscaping*, with cartoon goats pushing mowers and wielding rakes, edgers, and Weedwackers.

"Tim Darling just pulled in," Delaney said.

"He called yesterday when you were hunting." Allison stretched around the corner to the kitchen, holding out her mug for a refill. "He wants to see his Grand Prix." She disappeared around the corner and began restocking the rack.

Tim had his truck backed up to the pole barn and was unloading new wheels and tires from the bed.

"More wheels?" Delaney said. "What's wrong with the ones we put on it?" She walked through the side door of the barn and opened the bay door from inside.

"Not a thing," Tim said. "My dad used to have these same ones on his

Pontiac, and I got a good deal." He lifted the final wheel from the bed as if it were made of foam and stacked it on the others. Delaney knew Tim through his wife, Alice. For years, she would send Delaney Facebook invitations to join this or that "great business opportunity," which were obvious pyramid schemes. Those stopped when Alice opened a CrossFit gym out of one of Tim's company's garages. Her primary clientele was new mothers, and she used photos of her own "health journey" to keep the revenue stream rolling. Similarly, a decade of mowing lawns, clearing brush, plowing snow, and hauling deck stones had turned Tim into a tanned block of a person and an even tougher businessman. He'd bought up maintenance contracts and the competition until green GOAT trucks were everywhere.

"You're still on the hook for the ones we got," Delaney said.

"That's more than fair," Tim said. He walked to the back, rolling a wheel on either side of himself. "I'm happy to pay for any extra labor, too." He flashed the same smile Delaney recognized on billboards across the county. The one with his head cocked back and to one side as if the camera had caught him mid-laugh. Delaney made up a new invoice while Tim got the other wheels. She'd never been flush enough to spend as easily as Tim was now, and with how poorly the year was turning out for her, she did her best to stretch his eagerness. If it hadn't been for this old car, she was convinced she'd have gone under. A car horn spun her from the computer. Tim had climbed into the Grand Prix and waved at her from the driver's seat.

"It looks great!" he said. He honked again.

Out at the truck, Delaney handed Tim the new bill.

"$32,000," she said.

"How about a square thirty grand?" Tim replied, adding an arched eyebrow to his billboard smile.

"Thirty-two," she said. She projected confidence. Tim made a killing during the recession, contracting for banks that needed their foreclosed properties looking sellable. It was amazing that he could afford this piece of rebuilt history just from mowing lawns. But since he could, Delaney wasn't going to be shy about charging him.

"Well, it's worth it to have something to share with my daughter," he said.

Delaney and Allison had prime real estate in the line outside Goodwill. They needed Lacoste, Burberry, whatever filtered in from Macy's in Saginaw. More familiar brands were harder to come by. People knew what they were holding when they saw the tag, and who knew what the employees nabbed before it made it to the sales floor. Anything useful or collectible like little spoons from national parks or beer mugs from across the Midwest sold well. Power tools, always. The morning sun shone over the Goodwill sign and doves cooed from a nest made at the bottom of the *G*. The line stretched back to the next building over, the Gen-lectric field office. One of the office windows had been broken and covered with a stretch of plywood. A young man in khakis and a polo walked down the Goodwill line, offering pamphlets to those waiting for the store to open. He handed one to the sisters. It read, STOP BIG WIND.

"Follow the money," he said. "Who really benefits from those windmills?" Before they could read the pamphlet or respond, the man was in front of the field office giving it the middle finger. A sign posted above him on the building said, *Monitored by 24-Hour Video*.

Once inside Goodwill, their system was to work from the back of the store forward. After half an hour, they had some blouses, two cordless drills, and, cha-ching, a Princess House table lighter. On their second pass, Delaney stooped to rummage through the boxes under the clothing racks. Under tattered suitcases, three JFK commemorative plates, and a crate of vinyl records was a cardboard box cocooned in shrink wrap and plastered with stickers that said, *Country Style*. Delaney pulled out her pocketknife, slitting the plastic to find salt and pepper shakers shaped like tiny mason jars. Fifty of them for five bucks. Sold. Christine at the diner would buy these off her.

The Corner Coffee Café was a Caro staple that had survived the previous decade on the same Gordon Food Service menu. Most people believed it was impossible to screw up breakfast, which the diner sold all day. Butter, salt, pork, potatoes, and eggs paired seven different ways for the Daily Specials priced at six bucks. Coffee a dollar-twenty-five, a quarter more than when the place was known as Downtown Diner up until 2009. Christine, the current and longest-serving owner, had hired a young local airbrush artist to fill the front window with seasonal murals. It was currently a pumpkin patch with the center pumpkin shaped like a coffee pot, the steam curling into leafy vines. Old Chevys and a couple long Buicks filled the parking spots outlining the corner.

Inside, up front by the windows, were three men nose-deep into the *Tuscola County Advertiser*, flipping, folding, and passing news stories over plates of home fries and scrambled eggs. One was middle-aged and the other two were old sugar beet farmers who, had they worked at anything else, would have long been retired. Delaney recognized the first man. Most people around Caro did. For years, Dick Finney was at the front of every crowd who gathered to protest anything from a raised school millage to removal of the courthouse nativity scene. Boomers loved him soldiering for the good ol' days, but Delaney believed he was simply trying to out-talk the rumors from a decade before. Something about a girl who Delaney had once played junior varsity volleyball against. The other men were always in the diner whenever Delaney came to sell to Christine. They were solving the problems of the universe, fueled by coffee and sausage and grape jelly sandwiches. Their waitress, in an apron and a Coffee Crew softball T-shirt that said *Lefty Lila* on the back, circled the table, refilling their mugs, regular in her left hand, decaf in her right. She stopped, poured, shuffled, and slid around the table like a ballet dancer on a football field, slipping untouched and un-coffee-stained between the men.

Christine was at the register and waved Delaney in, pointing to the kitchen. Delaney repositioned the case of shakers onto her hip like she would a toddler and sidestepped the tables into the kitchen while Allison nabbed a booth. A cook was scraping charred cheese off the flattop. He was Delaney's age and, like her, a dropout from various levels of education, trying to make life happen.

"Got something you're gonna love," Delaney said. She placed the shakers on a stainless-steel prep table and peeled back the shrink wrap.

"That doesn't look like a new hood system," Christine said. She pushed a sweaty tangle of hair behind her ear. Peering into the case, she laughed, snorting a little at the contents. "Those are darling. How much?"

"A dollar-fifty per. Seventy-five total."

"I'll do sixty."

"Amazon sells them for ninety. My site would list them at eighty-five."

Christine raised an eyebrow. "Well, at least you're giving me a discount." She patted Delaney's shoulder as she left the kitchen for the cash register. Passing around the breakfast counter, Delaney took the cash from Christine and slid into the booth across from Allison. Lila dropped a copy of the *Advertiser* in front of Delaney and flipped over the mug in front of her, pouring the rest of the pot, about half a cup. "Fresh will be up in five minutes," she said. She left the sisters with a menu and went back to the men up front.

"So, what's the plan for this month?" Allison asked. She took Delaney's half mug and began adding little cups of creamer from the bowl on the table.

"Same as every September, I guess," Delaney said. "You head back downstate to Mom's and Carl's, and I scour Goodwill."

"But unlike every other September, you're struggling." Allison stacked three empty creamer cups onto each other like a tiny pyramid.

"The Pontiac will help," Delaney said. "And there's still some emergency funds from Alton's life insurance." She pushed the menu to the edge of the table. She wasn't hungry and the thought of going into winter in the red didn't help her appetite.

"You know what I'm going to say," Allison said.

"Then don't say it."

"Change the company name," Allison said. "You got a golden ticket when Alton adopted you. You got the Southby name. Southby's Sundries rolls off the tongue!"

Allison had pushed this rebranding line at her before and Delaney didn't want any part of it. Before their mother, Jackie, had remarried and moved back to Detroit, before Allison was even a twinkle in Carl's eye, Delaney had lived with Alton Southby after the disastrous flood of 1986 had washed Jackie's home, and Delaney's father, away. Alton had saved Jackie from the flood, and news of that had spread, making him a hero across the county. Jackie had been pregnant with Delaney at the time, and when Alton found out, he didn't hesitate to offer up adoption to Jackie, despite being three decades older. News of this spread, making him a legend. He didn't even expect marriage from Jackie, and when news of *this* spread, he became elevated to saint.

Yes, Delaney shared the name, but for years she'd done well enough without having to rely on the reputation of county lawyers, big farmers, and the Patron Saint of Tuscola County himself. What Allison didn't know was that for the first fourteen years of Delaney's life, before Allison was born, their mother never slept a full night. Delaney would hear her sometimes talking in her sleep, thrashing her arms as if she were drowning in a watery nightmare. She moved when Delaney entered high school and was happy back in the city. Delaney didn't know whether to call it fate or pride, but she was determined to make a life where her mother couldn't, where her birth father had wanted to.

Delaney deflected. "You kinda got his name, too, *Al*lison."

"Har har," Allison said. Lila returned with fresh coffee but one of the men up front pulled her away.

"No, Dan, I'm telling you," one man said. It was Dick Finney. Delaney rolled her eyes at Allison. "They are putting in bigger ones. Bigger and louder," Dick continued.

"Bigger don't mean louder, Dick," Dan said.

"The hell you mean 'bigger don't mean louder?'" Dick said. "This is America. Pull your head out of your ass."

"I'm with Dick," Derek said. "I've gone to a few of those Gen-lectric meet and greets. I thought Mr. Bellows was gonna murder a man when one of the 'community sponsors' said that close to seventy of those whopper turbines will be up and fully functional by the end of next year."

"Their noise drives people insane," Dick said. "I'm proof of that. I haven't had a good night's sleep in close to a decade." The table groaned at this.

"Rid Bellows Sr. ain't got a horse in this race," Dan said. "His land is too low to the river to qualify for wind, even if he wanted it. He'd know that if he did more listening than talking."

"He was going on about them being fire hazards, lightning rods," Derek said. "Made a bit of sense if you think about it."

"They're grounded," Dan said. "They rarely catch fire."

"Well, the Democrats hogtied us," Dick said. The table groaned louder.

"Shut it," Dick said. He folded a sausage link into a slice of toast and stuffed half of it into his mouth.

Allison used her hands to mimic two mouths talking at each other. She stuck her tongue out and crossed her eyes as the men rambled on.

"Remember when everyone was up in arms when those massive cell towers went up?" Dick Finney said. "Well folks took their foot off the gas and now everyone and their toddler has a smartphone. The Thumb ain't been the same since. People are tired. No wonder Trump won and is gonna win again."

"What, exactly, did the Democrats tie us to?" Dan stabbed at his omelet. "Gen-lectric paid for the road improvements and our taxes haven't gone up, even when these bigger blades started coming in and the county had to widen the intersections out in the country."

"Look, gentleman, front page," Dick said. The whole table, synchronous, like school children, turned to the front page of the *Advertiser*. Listening in, Delaney opened her paper and spun it around so both her and Allison could read. "There it is in full color."

On the cover was a half-page photo of a country road, newly paved, cutting through a wheat field. It was Delaney's road. She recognized her mailbox. Dividing the photograph was a single wind turbine blade. Sleek and impossibly white, it extended from before the left side of the frame, well beyond the right, as if it went on forever. Above the frame read, "Big[ger] Changes Planned Through 2020." Dick dropped the paper onto the table, pinning it down with his fist. The headline didn't seem to tell much of a story, Delaney thought. Change what? Turbines had been coming into the Thumb for close to a decade. Allison scanned the article and found that the leases signed by landowners covered any lost crop revenue. More so if the land could host multiple turbines. She had to turn to page A7 to find that, though.

"That's just the headline," Allison said, loud enough for the men to hear. They shifted their gazes to the sisters.

"What more do you need to know?" Dick said.

"The land the energy company uses is leased by the landowners," Delaney added.

"Yeah, been years of them tearing up our land to put up them eyesores."

Dick spread grape jelly on a slice of toast. "Or was that a little before your time, sweetheart?"

"Guess your eyes are starting to go," Allison replied. She turned toward him and sipped her coffee. "Or don't you know what 'Story Continues on A7' means?" Dick munched on his toast, a splotch of purple in the corner of his mouth.

"I know you," he said. He pointed at Delaney. "You're that gal who tried selling old photos of people around town. You remember her, Derek?" The beet farmer piled eggs on a butter-drenched slice of Texas toast. He shrugged. "Yeah, you do. We all remember her. This time last year, she was front page news."

"Artistic expression is protected by the First Amendment," Delaney said. She'd rehearsed this response in her head for months, but this was the first time she had actually said it out loud. What was legal and what was moral didn't always match up. Then add in the need to pay bills and the mismatch grew even more. People didn't seem to want to understand that, though. Or they were too caught up with how right and wrong impacted their own lives that they forgot simple things like how different people survive. "You said it yourself: This is America."

"Hijacking family photos ain't art," Dick said. "I told the boys here just as much."

"They were for sale," Delaney said. "And you weren't the judge."

"Just because a court lets you off, don't make you right," Dick said. "You stole people's history, cut it all up, and tried making a buck off it."

"A lot of talk about stealing history from the guy who stole someone's future," Allison said. "Or are we also too young to know about that, *Killer?*" Dick shot up from his chair, but the two farmers pulled down on his arms. Allison had only been a kid when Dick first made the news, a long night of drinking turned violent. But those stories stuck.

"If you knew what you were talking about, you'd know how stupid a comment that was," Dick said.

"You're right," Allison said. "I suppose you were found not guilty." She turned to Delaney. "Wasn't somebody just talking about the court not knowing right from wrong?"

"Let's go," Delaney said. "We've got inventory to log."

"Still at it, eh?" Dick said.

"At what? Trying to make a living?" Delaney didn't look at him as she stood at the register.

"If you wanna call it that," Dick said.

"You need some sugar for that bitter coffee?" Allison asked.

"Two-fifty," Christine said.

"Here's ten," Delaney said.

"Their coffee is on us," Allison said.

―――

In the early stages of turbine construction, a truck had backed out of the wheat field onto Delaney's half acre, leaving long ruts in her side yard. She'd seen it as an opportunity to finally use the spare lumber she'd scored at an estate sale earlier that summer. Allison masked over the deep, muddy scars with raised box gardens. They looked so damn good that Delaney earmarked "lumber" in her "Estate Sale MUSTS" spreadsheet. Allison had spent that summer building garden boxes and Delaney posted them with the caption, "Elevate your gardening." Priced $150–$200 and practically zero overhead because who really tried reselling old wood when they were clearing out houses? Pretty useless as is, Delaney thought.

After logging the day's haul into inventory and posting new pictures to the site, Delaney headed out to the gardens. She enjoyed spending the evenings outside with the expanse of fields stretching in every direction, the turbine behind the barn, and the dozens dotting the horizons, spinning and whooshing in the orange evening. She felt like she was at the center of the world plucking ripe tomatoes and wide basil leaves. Allison pulled the stained rocker out to the gardens along with a rag and wood polish. She sat in it and began rubbing at its arms. Delaney pinched a handful of basil, herby sweetness wafting in the air. She handed a smaller tomato and some basil to her sister who grabbed them with her teeth, juices running down her chin, not stopping her polishing. Deer grazed along the tree line on the other side of the wheat field, the turbine spinning above them. Most nights when Allison was home, they stayed out long enough to hear the slow, deliberate whine of the yaw as the shifting wind turned the turbines in unison.

"How long is this going to last?" Allison asked.

"What?"

Allison pointed to the rocker then to the barn. "Delaney's Discounts," Allison said.

Delaney didn't answer. She didn't have another plan, didn't think up this resale thing as a stopgap until another life began. This was it.

"I see the books, Del," Allison continued. "You're overstocked and undersold."

"We get paid."

"I know." She pushed her thumbnail along the armrest, years of black gunk curling and falling into the grass. "No hard feelings, Del," Allison said, "but this ain't my life. I help because I love you. Not because you pay me."

Delaney shook soil from a few radishes and dropped them into the basket at her feet. When she got her license, Allison started driving up to work summers with Delaney, returning before the school year started. Now that she was a sophomore at Wayne State taking full loads every semester, her summers were shorter.

"It's been slow, yeah," Delaney said.

"You only logged half a dozen items before our Goodwill trip."

"Sometimes people are too attached to sell," Delaney said. She used her pocketknife to trim leaves from a row of leaf lettuce.

"You know why that is," Allison said. "Gimme your knife." Delaney finished the row and passed it over. Allison used the back of the blade to scrape more age out of the corners of the chair.

"The lawsuit was dropped," Delaney said.

"Yeah, but those diner flies had a point. People don't want to feel like they're being used. They want to feel like they're part of something."

"You learn that at college?"

"We all want to feel like we belong," Allison said. "Shit, this chair is filthy. I'll finish later. Let's eat before I lose my appetite."

———

Delaney was making a habit of sleeping horribly. Which she then worried over in and of itself. Being too tired to work compounded into missed opportunities and missed opportunities meant missed money and missed money meant no house payment, no food, no future. In bed, in the dark, she could see this straight road of failure and her barreling down it with no brakes. She kicked off her comforter and sat on the edge of her bed. A grinding roar came from outside, like a dying robot, and Delaney pulled open the curtains. There was nothing to see in the moonless dark across the field. The only thing out there that could make such a racket was the turbine. She tossed on a hoodie as she went down the hall, leaving Allison asleep.

At the edge of the property, the outline of the turbine came into focus as her eyes adjusted to the dark. It had not stopped spinning but the grinding was louder. A bloom of orange and red popped from the housing atop the tower, followed by a shrieking, shaking explosion. Fire curled down the tower and along the three blades. With each rotation, flames flung from the tips of the blades and into the dry wheat field. A second explosion rocked from the base of the tower and the structure began to sway. Between it and the property, a patch of wheat began to smolder and catch. Delaney ran to it, using her hoodie to smother the flame. A blade fell from the rotor and its slow, heavy momentum threw it toward Delaney. It sunk deep into the earth, the soil wrapping around it like a hand closing around a sword's hilt. Deep oranges spiraled against the night. The keening metal buckled halfway up the tower and the structure collapsed down onto itself before tipping toward Delaney. She backed away, fumbling to the ground. From over the tops of the wheat, she watched the turbine fall, metal wailing. She rolled over, pressing herself to the dry earth, looking back at the approaching disaster. The turbine hit the ground, causing another explosion to rocket from the nacelle. Smoldering debris pelted the ground around Delaney. She rolled over to face the destruction, afraid to be hit from behind. A wall of flames spread from the engulfed wreckage and shards of machinery shot from it, arching high then falling to the field like meteors.

She pushed herself forward to her feet, running through the smoke and wheat dust, the smell of oil and wheat choking her, small patches of fire growing across the field. In her backyard, a wash of pain bit into her foot and she fell. A charred hunk of metal sat smoking in the grass. The bottom of her sock had burned away and the sole of her foot was black.

More hunks dotted the yard, and Delaney had to hopscotch her way back to the house. The center of the back porch smoldered and a thick line of smoke curled from the roof of the house. Allison met her at the back door and Delaney fell into her.

"Fire department is on the way," Allison said. She propped up her sister and they three-leg raced to the driveway then down the newly paved road.

They made it to the next intersection and watched a wall of fire creep around their house. Sirens and blue and red flashes stretched across the expanse of midnight fields.

———

The headline in the papers the morning after the explosion read, "Too Close For Comfort"? A week later the headlines read, "Accident or Arson?" Two weeks later, it was determined that, yes, it had been a purposeful attack. But that information was buried in a thick Sunday edition along with the news that Delaney's house was gone but fire departments from Akron, Caro, and Fairgrove had been able to save the pole barn.

One month after the explosion, Delaney pulled into her driveway, running over the police tape feathered across the gravel. The foundation of her house was still sound, an inspector had told her, but rebuilding plans were on a horizon too far away, too expensive to reach. If an arson investigation led to an arrest, then she'd have a line on a civil suit. She could call the Southby cousins who were attorneys in Cass City, the ones who'd kept inviting her to Easter dinner even after Alton died. But an arrest was a big *if*; it seemed nobody was in the finger-pointing mood, as if the whole countryside had banded together to lash out at the invading world, then keep themselves safe from the fallout.

In the meantime, Delaney had converted the pole barn into a type of apartment. The canvas tarp that once covered the old photographs now hung in the back where the Pontiac used to be and made a mostly private sleeping nook. Behind the tarp, she had strung up a camping hammock she had scored at a garage sale. The barn drew water from a well and she had a dozen garden hoses that hadn't sold. She was able to wash her hair, her foot, and the merchandise. She called that a win. She used a minifridge and a microwave she'd nabbed at an estate sale. Another win.

Six weeks after the explosion, Delaney had more prime real estate in the lineup outside Goodwill. She had skulked through the wreckage of her home, finding as many whole collectibles as she could. She'd recovered two Precious Moments, five blue glass birds, and one JFK commemorative plate. Allison had started school the week after the fire and was already back in Detroit. She told Delaney she wasn't sure if she was going to work the next summer. She planned to add a second major and might have to take summer courses. The way she said it, that 2020 was "too far off to tell," forced Delaney to plan for a future fully alone. Her foot had made steady progress after weeks of twice daily draining and rebandaging, but she still balanced it on the shopping cart in front of her. Her two nights in the hospital without insurance and the two follow-up appointments erased most of what selling the Pontiac brought in. Fiery pinpricks burrowed into her heel and up her leg. She fished half a Vicodin from her pocket and swallowed it dry. The doctors were confident that she'd get most of the feeling in her toes back and any limp wouldn't be noticeable. So, mostly, it would all be a wash. Christmas was the next big event in Delaney's calendar; no way would people not be looking for discounts. She could not bank on lawsuits or charity. She had to be ready to buy and sell.

The line behind her, by the Gen-lectric field office, was considerably louder—more a mob than a line. Another stretch of plywood covered a second window and graffiti covered both. One line in red, white, and blue read, *Globalists Go Home.* Another read, *MAGA.* A man in a red trucker hat walked the crowd, handing out yellow yard signs and chanting, "Too Close, Too Loud." Others held up the signs and chanted with him. He pushed one into Delaney's hands.

"You look like you could use a cup of coffee," he said. It was Dick Finney. "Extra sugar." Before Delaney could refuse the sign, he was gone, screaming at the surveillance camera propped above the office door.

The sign had a black image of a turbine with smoke billowing off it and the words, *NOT SO SILENT KILLERS.* It didn't matter that no one had died. It didn't matter that someone had done this on purpose. Despite what people said, what yard signs read, the turbines were huge but hundreds of yards away and when the blades spun to run perpendicular to the ground, it seemed as if someone could reach up and grab hold. They were like illusions. Magic.

That was their problem, Delaney thought. People believed they were too much of what, in reality, they weren't.

Streaks of White and Color

Kingston Tap opened at noon during the week. Leah Demers waited in the parking lot at quarter to. She'd bailed on a job interview at a print shop and didn't want to go back home to explain herself to her mother.

"Hey, Jamaica," Leah said. "Arrow and tonic."

"I know," the bartender said.

———

Marcy Cutler woke at six each morning and lay in bed wondering which part of herself she would hate that day. Her toes for their arthritis? Her legs for their blue river veins? Her voice for cracking when she goes out to Levon's memorial and wishes him good morning? Or would she end up hating the thing she loved to hate most: the voice in her head that lists the things about herself that she has grown bitter toward. She set her feet down and wiggled her toes. They cracked pain through her feet.

"Toes it is," she said.

Marcy's house sat three hundred yards back from Outer Road on the south edge of the Cass River. She was explicit when she had the first ash tree felled to start the clearing for the house: She wanted to live far enough away from the road so she didn't have to hear the roar of cars as they crossed Bucky's Bridge. But during her forty years in that house, cars got bigger and louder. Her old age was filled with echoes.

———

Jennifer came into Kingston Tap to give Leah the fifty dollars she owed her. Leah used ten of that to buy a round.

"Thanks again for posing," Leah said. Jennifer had modeled for her. "This is the first payday I've had in three weeks."

"Don't mention it," Jennifer said. "I like how being painted makes me feel." Rough drafts and copies of Jennifer's portrait sat under a bedsheet in Leah's mother's garage. Usually, payment was the other way around, the artist paying models for their time, but Leah was a couple years younger than her and, selfishly, Jennifer felt like a big sister. She loved her and wanted to help her succeed.

"You've got a good face," Leah said. "It's always fun to paint." She pointed to Jennifer, her finger tracing a figure eight in the air.

"You'll be at tomorrow's memorial, right?" Jennifer said.

"Of course. Got something special I've been working on."

"Something special?"

"You'll find out tomorrow," Leah said. "It's probably the best work I've done in years."

Jennifer leaned in and hugged Leah. "I know it will be great," she said. She felt Leah's fingers press into the grooves where her shoulder blades flared out.

"I've got some final details to iron out," Jennifer added, getting up to leave. She pointed to the bar where two empties sat in front of her friend. "Hey, Jamaica," she said to the bartender, "don't let her stay here all day."

The bartender gave her a thumbs-up as Jennifer left.

Every year, Jennifer gathered the gang to remember her sister, Paisley, who'd been killed at a backwoods bar in what the state of Michigan had deemed "manslaughter." The men responsible had varying forms of justice levied against them, all of which Jennifer found lacking. Better to celebrate a life than to ruminate, she had told herself year after year. It had taken her the last decade to get somewhat comfortable with that notion.

Leah felt the bones of her Chevy Blazer shaking as she sailed through the stop signs north of Bucky's Bridge. She saw that the corn in the fields was only ankle high. Anyone, drunk or otherwise, could see oncoming cars a half mile before crossing any intersection. Leah wasn't looking for other cars, though. She was just lucky upon lucky with each passing red sign. She was halfway to nowhere in the middle of the afternoon on a Tuesday, when farmers were in from the fields, when kids were in school, when people were where they said they'd be.

The Blazer had been a gift from her father when he divorced her mother and moved to Chicago. He'd been good to it, made sure it ran easy, like a deep breath. *She's got another hundred-thousand miles left in her*, he'd written on the note he left on the dash. *Drive her until she dies.* Leah loved the car and as a kid grew up planning the ways she'd put her mark on it. Two months after her dad left, she painted it. On the hood was a tree grown into the shape of a woman, the forest spreading out under the breadth of her limbs. Birds playing in her hair, squirrels nestled under her chin. From her canopy, daylight washed back down the driver's side, illuminating the tops of other trees, of deer, raccoons, of a hunter propped against a boulder, asleep. Nighttime spread down the passenger's side, coating a pond surrounded by honeysuckle and raspberry bushes. A skunk and her kits crowded at the water's edge under the back door window. She'd sketched it over and over in her notebooks, on napkins, on her calf once.

She'd shown it off the past five years at Cars and Crafts Weekend. People stopped. Stared. Complimented her on the seasonal murals she had painted in various storefronts and restaurants. She had business cards some people took, and some even paid fifteen dollars for a quick portrait she whipped out on the back of index cards. There were cash prizes for loudest engine and one for smokiest peel out. There was no prize money for best paint job.

"You can't paint food onto the table for your kids," her mother always told her.

"I don't have kids," Leah always said. "Don't want them."

Marcy's husband, Levon, had died a year earlier. Overworked himself at a small tool and die shop until he was more pain than man. He began worrying about Bucky's Bridge with his extra time, who might be living under it, who treated it like part of some racetrack. When it got to where he couldn't even patrol the area with his Army-issued flashlight anymore, Marcy would take shorter walks with him through the woods. He picked up birdwatching but hadn't learned anything beyond *robin, mourning dove,* and what he called *hey theres*, because to him, that's what it sounded like they were saying.

"Those are chickadees," she'd tell him.

"Hey there, chickadee," he'd reply.

"That's more stupid than cute," she'd say, squeezing his hand.

He called this, with a smile, a veteran's death, and when it came for real, Marcy built a memorial at the edge of their woods where the land fell away to the river. It was a bird feeder with LEVON carved into the post and a smiley face made out of the O.

She kept his remains in a gray clay urn on a catchall in the breezeway. He held down coupon books and junk mail. Marcy caught herself a few too many times hanging her keys on the nub on top of the urn's lid. He'd been good at keeping himself busy when he was alive but now that he was dead, Marcy didn't know what to do with him. The birds took to the memorial and a notion came to Marcy, something unjustifiable but perfect. On warm afternoons, she hauled a camp chair out to the bird feeder, said a rosary, and sprinkled some of Levon's ashes into the seed. She'd begun to imagine that he had become a part of every bird she saw, and when a chickadee called from the shadow of some bough, it took everything she had not to call back.

Leah's tree woman kissed the guard rail of Bucky's Bridge then spun like a rifled bullet above the undergrowth that carpeted the riverbanks. Tops of trees snapped and fell to the water along with shattered glass and chipped paint. The windshield flew back into the cab as the Blazer soared out above the water. Warm, musky air trapped under the bridge gushed into the cab as it descended.

Marcy was filling Levon's bird feeder with seed and a dusting of Levon's ashes when she heard a concertina of metal on metal, metal on wood, then a thunderous splash of metal on water. It happened in the time it took Marcy to turn her head, and, focusing out from the overhang of the memorial, she saw leaves floating down to a crumpled mass half sunk in the middle of the Cass River. Her heart choked her. So, it had finally happened, she thought, just like Levon said it would. Someone had finally learned the hard way that Outer Road wasn't a raceway. She was dizzy with the image and ran to the edge of the overhang. Sliding down the steep bank, her feet screamed as she reached the bottom.

Despite Marcy's quick 911 call, the woman pulled from the car was unresponsive. Police on the scene said the Blazer must've hit beyond ninety miles per hour when it plowed into the guard rail. The initial impact was enough to kill most people. This didn't take into account, they said, the half dozen trees the vehicle took out, each thick enough to turn a car into not a car. One firefighter chimed in that it also didn't consider the final impact. Marcy listened to the workers talk as a clean-up crew chopped through undergrowth and trees to clear a path to retrieve the wreckage.

"If you're going to go," one deputy said, "this wouldn't be the slowest."

"I pray it was quick," another said.

—

Leah died slowly from drowning, feeling like she was on the cusp of something wonderful. She was a bit chilly, but coldness made her think of freshness. She figured she was dreaming and was scared that, when she woke up, she'd still be tired, unemployed, and drunk.

—

The gang met at Kingston Tap on Wednesday to start their memorial evening. Paisley would've been thirty that year but who knows for sure how she would have wanted to celebrate. That was the bitch of it, Jennifer believed, the older she got, the less confident she became with what she thought her younger sister would have wanted. The first memorial had been huge. Old high school friends came back from college, family came into town, and Jennifer's parents had rented out the Knights of Columbus Hall. They'd even raised money for a local substance abuse nonprofit. As the years passed, though, fewer high school friends returned. After a particularly thin turnout, Jennifer's parents had removed themselves from involvement, saying it was too hard to see how easy it was for a small town to forget one of its own. For the last two years, the only ones who showed up to celebrate Paisley's life had been her, Leah, Colton Darling, and John Erskine. They all had been at Colwood Bar the night Paisley was killed. Colton had even subdued one of the men responsible.

Colton picked at a bowl of pretzels and John flipped through the newspaper at their corner table. Jennifer was at the bar getting the first round. A small dinner crowd began filling the place. Maybe this was all it needed to be, Jennifer thought. To be remembered by a handful of people who had seen you through to the end.

"You seen Leah?" she asked Jamaica.

"Yesterday, same as you," Jamaica said. She poured foam from the first pint, leaving it set while she started on the second. At the table, the men declared that if Jamaica didn't have an answer, nobody did.

"Leah's phone just goes to voice mail," Colton said.

"I'm sure she's in her mom's garage painting," John added. "You know how focused she gets when she goes full-on artist mode."

Colton blew a raspy whistle and drank.

"I guess you're right," Jennifer said.

"Here, have some pretzels," Colton said.

"Have you two seen the news?" John said. He pushed the newspaper to the center of the table.

———

When Katherine Demers opened her front door and saw two cops, her first emotion was a familiar, dull anger, the kind that cut into her guts, leaving them twisted. She assumed when her daughter hadn't come home she was sobering up on a concrete bench behind bulletproof glass. So much for the interview at the screen-printing shop, Katherine thought. Now she'd have to call up her friend there and apologize and lie for Leah. *You know how those artsy types are*, she'd say. Yeah, that was a good one. Yeah, that was a reliable one.

The deputies asked her if she was familiar with a '98 Blazer with a custom paint job. Of course she was, everyone was. She said she'd meet the deputies at lockup to bail her daughter out. She knew the routine.

"We actually need you to ride in with us," one deputy said.

On the ride into town, the deputies offered canned responses to every question Katherine asked.

"I swear," Katherine said, "I barely recognize Leah when she pulls this shit. I'm sorry for all of this. I really am. I raised her better. But you know how those artsy types are, right?" She clasped her hands and hunched over her lap. Her shoulders sank and shame trickled down her arms like beads of sweat. She used to blame Leah's actions on her father leaving them, but that excuse wore thin before that year was out. Katherine leaned her head on the window and watched cows graze as the cruiser passed by.

———

"Single-car Crash Takes Area Woman," read the front page of the *Tuscola County Advertiser*.

"Fake news," Colton said, peering at the dateline: Friday, September 20, 2019. "No way that's true."

Colton and John scoured the paper for more information. They found a small color photograph of a crumpled SUV being winched up a riverbank.

"There it is, man," John said. "Says authorities believe alcohol was a factor."

"They gotta say that even if the person only had one beer," Colton said. "Blood alcohol ain't an accurate measure. Leah holds her own." He paged through to the obituaries.

It was early, the sun halfway down the evening side of the sky. A couple sat at a short table, cracking at peanuts in a basket. Two cooks clanged spatulas against the service window and waitresses slid from table to bar and back again with trays of burgers and beers. "See? Nothing about Leah in the obituaries."

"Don't be stupid," John said. "The news don't work that fast. Jennifer, call Katherine. Chances are Leah's sleeping it off in lockup."

The edges around the headline blurred into a tunnel of streaking lights as Jennifer read and reread until the words didn't hold any meaning. *Single-car Crash Takes Area Woman. Takes.* Jennifer formed that word slowly, feeling how it pulled at the corner of her mouth, almost like a smile. *Taken.* As in stolen, a theft that Jennifer had suffered from once before. This wasn't possible. Not Leah, too. Not today.

"Earth to Jennifer," Colton said, snapping his fingers in the negative space between her eyes and the newspaper.

"We need to go there," she said.

"To Katherine's?" Colton said.

"To Bucky's Bridge," Jennifer said.

"Why?"

Takes. Taken. A theft of life. Jennifer tried to shake the images from her head. The photo of the wreck, though, brought back the image of Paisley convulsing and contorted, of Colton grappling that man to the ground, and of Leah's tears as she helped Jennifer into the back of the ambulance.

"I need to see where it happened," she said.

———

Marcy had been at Levon's memorial for hours. There was rustling down at the river, and she leaned around the trees, trying to see if it was raccoons she was hearing or maybe a family of deer. A woman yelled and something splashed into the water. Marcy stood up and listened. Levon told her he'd scared kids from under the bridge every once in a while. Sometimes he came home from a walk with empty spray paint cans. She wasn't about to claw her way down the embankment, though, not to follow some strangers into the darkness.

"You're on private property," she called. She heard more rustling and someone shushing someone else. Then nothing. "I know you heard me."

"We're friends of Leah," a woman's voice called. Marcy recognized the name from the newspaper.

"I didn't ask who you are," she said. "I told you where you are."

"We want to see where she went," the woman said.

"You can see better in daylight," Marcy said. "And from the bridge. That's my property down there and I won't be held responsible for any kind of accident or assholery you get into."

There was more rustling. Another small splash. Fine, Marcy thought. Fine, she'd be the bad guy.

"The next voice you hear will be the police," she called. She tapped her phone: no service. She fell back into her chair and waited. "I guess I should find your flashlight, huh?" she said to Levon's bird feeder. "Start patrolling like you used to."

She heard bodies climbing up the embankment. They were muttering, probably cursing the grumpy old lady in the dark, but if people wanted to grieve, let them do it the right way, Marcy thought. And that sure wasn't on the banks of some backwoods river in the middle of the night. And on private property of all things.

———

Two nights later, John parked his truck on state land set off Outer Road, roughly half a mile south of Bucky's Bridge. He pulled a plastic Walmart bag from the back seat and from that, two cans of glitter green spray paint, slotting them into the empty spaces of a six-pack. He crept along the shoulder until he reached the river, where he stood for a moment and listened. It was past midnight, no way that old lady was still up. He made his way down to the river's edge, keeping an ear toward the woman's house. Who did she think she was, anyway, telling the gang they couldn't send their friend off the right way? Over a decade ago, they'd done the same thing at Colwood Bar and nobody had said anything.

He heard rustling in the undergrowth then saw a deer slip into the river and swim across. He lost sight of it in the dark expanse of the river. Under the bridge were large flood boulders covered in faded graffiti. The green paint quickly covered old hearts and lovers' initials as John sprayed it along the side of bridge. In minutes, he had obliterated countless years of doodles that bored teenagers had probably forgotten about.

LEAH now stretched fifteen feet across the concrete and at least five feet high. John stepped back to see his work and cracked another beer.

"You went too heavy with the paint," Leah said. "It's going to run." She sat on one of the boulders, swinging her legs over its edge.

"Well excuse me," John said. "You're the artist. And a hallucination." He chugged his drink and let the can fall to the ground.

"Depends on if you think I'm here or just in your head," she said. She pointed at the paint can. "Hold it farther away from the canvas."

"I'm doing my best." John cocked his head from side to side. The paint had in fact run, and the *H* looked as if it were standing on stilts.

"How does that look?" He dropped the paint and cracked another beer alone in the dark.

———

The next morning, Marcy walked down the path the recovery crew had cleared. It was practically a highway for jerkoffs to use to congregate under the bridge. Empty Icehouse cans littered the bank. A couple fresh logs had been positioned along the base of the bridge. A hunk of blue windshield sat on one of them and a plastic bag was wedged under the other. Marcy grabbed the bag and began collecting the cans. She went for the glass but stopped, her attention drawn to the abutment. Someone had sprayed, in glitter green paint, LEAH LIVES ON. Marcy threw her hands up, her mouth hanging.

———

Jennifer called Katherine a dozen times over the next week. Each message she left was more emotional than the last until she'd started getting mad.

Listen, Kat, she was our family, too. You don't have any right keeping us from saying goodbye. You're being a real bitch, her last one said.

Katherine didn't understand how this worked, Jennifer thought. This wasn't right, and she would know. Keeping loved ones locked out only tied them to their grief.

———

Colton and John met in the parking lot of the medical care facility and waited for Jennifer to get off work.

"You been out there this week?" John asked.

"Yeah," Colton said. "You see the trees?"

"I didn't know they could twist like that," John said. They leaned on the front of John's truck and watched as aides wheeled two patients onto a corner of the parking lot laid with landscape stones and planted flowers. The two patients smiled up toward the sun. They were in bathrobes and sunglasses, the big kind that go over regular glasses. One aide went back inside, and the other pulled out their cell and sat on the stones.

"Wanna hear something screwed up?" Colton asked.

John checked his phone. "Make it wait, man. There's Jennifer." They got into his truck and pulled up to the entryway.

"Katherine's still not picking up," she said. "Her number rings once, then nothing." She tapped her nails along the window. "It's been a week. There won't be a funeral. I'll bet you."

It was the first weekend when college kids were home and the Run between all the country bars got busy early, just like it always had. Truck beds full of polos and sundresses sped north into the countryside, passing the gang as they pulled into Kingston. It was packed.

"I'm out," Jennifer said. "I can't drink with a bunch of college kids. Let's go."

"Every place is going to be the same," John said. Jennifer put a hand on his thigh and sunk her nails into his jeans.

"I can't," she said.

They went back to the Walmart in Caro and each bought a six-pack. They drank one on the way to Outer Road. It was dusk when they got to Bucky's Bridge.

"Do you think that lady is gonna be around?" Colton asked.

"Who cares?" John said. "We're grieving." He drove to the same state land lot he'd parked at earlier in the week. Mosquitoes drifted around them on the walk back and as they slipped back down the embankment.

It was darker at the river, the water already black, whirling around the bridge supports. A fish jumped upriver. Two geese hunkered next to each other on the opposite bank. The gang drank another round and shuffled around, taking turns looking out to where the Blazer had landed and at the scars in the mud from where it was dragged out. John rummaged around in the brush. He brought some wood into the clearing and began breaking it up.

"Might as well get comfortable," he said.

Jennifer scanned the clearing. The bluing evening light stripped away the shadows and it felt wide open, empty. It disgusted her.

"This doesn't feel right," she said. She started back up to the road.

"We just got here," Colton said.

"Leah is supposed to be here," she said.

The Demers' house was four miles north of Bucky's Bridge on a dirt back-road. There was enough cloud cover to block any moonlight and keep the gang hidden. Still, Jennifer had John cut his headlights and creep onto the shoulder.

"We need to walk the rest of the way," she said.

"Why don't we just knock on the front door?" John said. "If Katherine won't talk on the phone, maybe she'll talk face-to-face."

"If it were my kid, I'd drink until I couldn't feel feelings anymore," Colton said. "I'd be passed out."

"If it were me, the last thing I'd want to do is sleep," John said. "Think of the nightmares."

Jennifer gave them credit, they were both half right about grieving. The full truth was losing someone close was crazy-making. There was no end to the constant turning to speak to whomever was gone only to be met with the hole in the universe where they should have been.

"If I have to see Katherine, I might do something I regret," Jennifer said. "We're here for Leah's art, nothing else. We'll sneak into the garage and take a few paintings."

"I didn't sign up for any stealing," John said.

"It isn't stealing," Jennifer said. "She'd been working on something for Paisley's memorial. All we're doing is taking what is ours anyway."

They slid out of the truck and pressed the doors closed. It was humid and the air hung on their lips.

The house sat in the middle of a farmer's field. Struggling corn shoots soaked in the water puddles where the field bordered the driveway. The light over the front porch was on.

"What's that?" Colton said, pointing to a heap at the end of the driveway.

Jennifer gasped as they approached the entry to the drive.

Stacked at the side of the road were four massive cardboard boxes. On the front of one, someone, most likely Katherine, had written FREE in thick black marker. Jennifer rummaged through one, then another. They were filled with paint hoppers, lengths of tubing, spray nozzles, and paint cans. Unused canvas rolls poked from the boxes like dead tree trunks.

"It's all of Leah's art supplies," Jennifer said, her voice giving out.

"Check this out," Colton said. On the far end of the heap was a bed-sheet. He pulled it back to reveal dozens of canvases.

Jennifer propped up the top one and used her phone to light it. She flipped through more, revealing Leah's practice drafts. So many eyes stared back at the gang. Hazels, grays, blues.

Some had irises painted to reflect scenes from around the county. The failed dam across the Cass River where kids fished and teenagers tried to muscle through the current. The naked woman in the martini glass painted on the side of the old Colwood Bar. A field filled with wind turbines. Thick woods with deer peeking around the trees. Downtown Caro with boarded-up storefronts mixed in with others that featured miniature versions of Leah's own work.

Jennifer had never seen these before. It was as if she were reading her friend's diary, seeing how Leah saw the places that made up where they called home. At the bottom of each eye, Leah had written the date and the same short note: *Blink and It's Gone. 2008, 2010, 2016.* The newest written in 2019. There was no telling if she'd finished it weeks or even days before.

"We're taking these, too," Jennifer said, handing two to Colton. The next canvases were early versions of what had eventually made it onto Leah's Blazer. Jennifer lost her breath when she got to the last painting.

"Oh my God," she said. She fell backward, canvases crashing to the ground. Colton shushed them.

"Let me see," John said.

Jennifer hunched over a painting of two women. Their faces in black, white, and shades of gray on a brilliant rainbow background.

"Whoa," John said. "It's you."

"And Paisley," she said. Or, she thought, an image of what her sister might have looked like at thirty. Jennifer ran a finger along Paisley's nose, following it to where the right nostril flared out just a little too much, where her sister had a scar. A small detail that Leah had remembered.

"Holy shit," Colton said, crouching next to them. Leah had covered the canvas in a gradient of colors, blues and purples rising to oranges and yellows. The gray shadows behind the women's heads seemed to fall back into the canvas and the crisp lines of their necks and cheeks made the white spaces pop out as if the women were rising up to meet the gang.

"She was really good," John said.

"How dare Katherine just throw these away," Jennifer said. She began walking toward the house. "I'll never forgive her."

"She's not thinking straight," John said. He stepped in front of her. "Give her a break."

"Screw her," Jennifer said. "Katherine's just like every other dumb redneck living in this fucking county. No appreciation for art, no respect for the artist even when it's her own kid." She tried wrestling out of John's grasp, but he wrapped her in a hug.

"We're living in this county, too," he said, squeezing her.

"Guys, look," Colton said, pointing to the house.

The front porch light had been turned out.

———

Katherine hardly remembered what sleep was like. She sat in her living room every day, ignoring the phone and the doorbell. On the coffee table were small piles of forms, police and coroner reports, business cards from Randolph Funeral Home in Caro and Eastman's Funeral Services in Cass City. There's big business in dying, she thought, and no money to pay for it.

If only she'd forced her daughter to get her life together. Get a real job. She wouldn't have been at Bucky's Bridge on a goddamned Tuesday. She would be alive.

She heard rustling outside then a voice yelling. It was Jennifer. No doubt about it. Her sharp voice had lived in her voice mail box for days. She was yelling something about not getting to say goodbye.

If the curtains had been opened, she'd be able to turn and stare right at her daughter's friends. She snorted. Some friends, she thought. Drinking buddies. Enablers. Just as guilty for Leah's death as herself.

She turned out the front porch light then curled into the worn couch cushions, wishing she could ball her body up so tight that she'd pop out of existence. No way she'd sleep tonight, either.

Sleep was for the innocent.

———

Later that night, Marcy had a garbage bag half full of the junk the gang had strewn across the clearing. Beer cans, chip bags, and McDonald's fry containers. They'd even started a fire one of the nights and it looked like they were ready to start another one whenever they returned. They were like filthy pilgrims, drifting out to what was supposed to be her little patch of paradise. It might not be as isolated as she used to think, and Levon wasn't the best company anymore, but it was hers. Was that too much to ask for? She heard feet on the pavement and voices from the bridge. They were coming back twice the same night? This was too much. Marcy backed under the bridge, ducking behind the flood boulders.

The shadows came down the path. Marcy saw their outlines and large swathes of white that reflected every bit of twilight. She squinted to see what they were but couldn't make anything out. One shadow walked to the center of the clearing and pawed into a paper bag. A cell light came on and a white beam cast across the ground to the edge of the river. The figure pulled a plastic bottle from the bag and squeezed its contents onto the makeshift firepit. A lighter flicked and the bag caught before it fell to the pit. A flash of orange flame flew from the ground. The light shone on the face of a young man. Marcy didn't know him but watched him feed the flame. The others came into the light, a man and woman. The second man dragged two large logs closer to the fire and sat. He pulled a beer from a plastic ring and passed it to the woman. She had the white swathes, posters of some kind, leaning against her thighs, and the swaying firelight showed dozens of—Marcy tried to focus her vision. Were those eyes on the posters?

"Move over," the woman said. She stretched her feet toward the flame and rested her head on his shoulder. "Put a big one on," she said to the second man. He tossed a half-wet log into the flames and it hissed and smoked. He pulled the sleeves of his hoodie down and sat opposite her. They stayed quiet, watched the fire, and drank. The first round went fast, and the wet log finally caught, spreading the circle of light into focus. The posters were actually paintings, Marcy saw. The woman held one with two women and a rainbow on it.

"So, uh, wanna hear something screwed up?" the first man said.

"You asked that earlier today," the second man said.

"And you told me to wait, and I can't wait no more."

"Say it," the woman said.

"The sheriff's office had me wreck out Leah's Blazer this week," he said. "I had it all loaded in the crusher and—" he began sniffling, coughing to keep himself from crying. "And that tree on the door, with the face? I started the crusher up and, and—" Here he dropped his head between his knees, the expanse of his shoulders heaving like a slow earthquake. "God help me, but I saw that tree turn into Leah. She even waved at me." He mimed a wave out over the dark water and broke down, trying to finish his story through sobs, trying to tell the others how he'd had to finish his shift, how he'd had three more cars flattened and stacked on top of Leah before lunch. He chucked his beer can and it was gone with the current.

"Jesus, Colton," the woman said. She propped one of the paintings on the log and wrapped both arms around the man.

"They shouldn't have made you do that," the second man said. "If they'd cared, they woulda had someone else take care of it." He got up and tossed another rotting log onto the fire. The smell of oil and mud puffed across the clearing and under the bridge. He grabbed two of the paintings and arranged them along their sitting logs. One was a forest in daylight shown from the radius of the fire, the other was a series of eyes.

To Marcy, it looked like some kind of ritual. Levon had once called them *satanic love-ins*. She had always hated when he used fear as a joke. Kids around these parts got bored from time to time, caused trouble, but nothing like this. No fire and murals of eyes.

"The truck should have exploded," the second man said. The woman choked on her beer, using her shoulder to wipe her lips.

"John, what's the matter with you?" the first man, Colton, said.

"Think about it," John said. "It woulda been better." He pried a burnt end of a log with his boot, lifting it onto its tip and letting it fall into the center of the fire. The woman punched him between the shoulder blades.

"Shut up," she said.

"I'm serious, Jennifer," he said. "You're gonna die no matter what and if you're gonna go violent, it's better to be gone by fire than water." He threw more wood into the flames. "You become something new when you burn. Drowning, though? You become a bloated version of yourself. Disfigured at best. Fish food at worst." He threw a rock into the current. "Nobody should have to die in a place like this."

They were silent then for what seemed like a lifetime.

"You want to know something stupid," Jennifer said. She hadn't let go of the rainbow painting since she'd sat down. "When Paisley died, I wanted to kill the men who killed her. When only one of them went to prison for it, I wanted to make the man who got off suffer." She went to the fire, tilting the painting in the light. "Leah tagged that redneck's house for weeks. Spray-painted all kinds of shit on the garage door and siding. Busted a few windows, even. It was petty and it was definitely illegal, but it was right. Still, it didn't make me feel any better."

"What's stupid about that?" Colton said.

Jennifer pinched her burning eyes, snot creeping from her nose. "Once, I was able to tell the difference between what was myself and what was only the hurt I felt. I learned that people go away. But I thought that I could do something to keep people from going away like how Paisley did. Like how Leah did. That's what's stupid."

"I don't follow," John said.

"It's about how they're remembered that matters," Jennifer said. "I mean, look at this." She held the painting out to the men. "Leah had more talent than any of us and what good did it do her?" She spun the painting toward the light.

She was right. Marcy was far off, but in the brilliant streaks of flames, she could see the care applied to the canvas. She had to admit, even as the winch dragged the truck through the river, she saw amazing detail in how day and night folded onto one another. The wreck was almost its own work of art.

"You can't think like that, Jen," John said.

"I'll think however I goddamn please," she said. "Get me a beer, Colt."

"You already have one," he said. They became quiet again. Sniffling at their thoughts. Wiping at their faces. Drinking.

This wasn't some kind of evil, Marcy thought. It was a wake, or at least the next best thing. Levon had gotten her spooked for no reason. Marcy's body ached, and even though she'd been mostly wrong about what these kids were doing, she still needed to break up the party. She checked her phone—almost one in the morning. She stepped over rocks and into the faded periphery of light.

"You're the ones who have been coming around, huh?" she asked. The gang jumped.

"You're the one who was yelling at us last week," Jennifer said.

"You're on my property, so I'll talk however I like," Marcy said.

"We're not doing anything," Jennifer said. "Leave us alone."

"And is that not doing anything?" Marcy said. She pointed at the LEAH LIVES ON graffiti.

"Ma'am, we're just, you know," John said, "trying to deal."

"I'm sorry about your friend, but this is no way to grieve," Marcy said. "There's right and wrong ways to do that."

"Don't talk to me about grief," Jennifer said. "Her name is Leah, and every time she pops into my head, it's not images of her painting anymore. It's not memories of our lives together. I think of her dying out here. I can't stop thinking it. Playing out how it might have went. In my mind, it's like she's dying over and over again and I can't do anything to stop it." She kicked a log and sparks flew into the dark like tiny birds. "So, if she's dying over and over again, lady, then how are we supposed to grieve?"

Marcy started as if she had an answer to this. She thought she would. She wanted to tell this woman how she didn't have the first clue what the truth of life and death was. That every morning hurt a little less in the heart but a little more in the bones and every night was a bit smaller than the one before. Grief was slow and quiet and that's just the way it had to be. Levon's ashes still filled most of his urn, at least five more years' worth of bird feeding left before he was gone gone.

"Look," Colton said. "Can we have tonight? We'll keep it down."

The three of them, and the paintings, stared at Marcy. They were begging her. It felt like they were silently screaming their case. Bats circled out over the water, feeding.

Marcy pulled the plastic rings of a six-pack from between two rocks and began ripping the circles apart. The can John had thrown was too far into the water for her to reach. Folks who have no choices end up making mostly dumb ones, Marcy thought. Being young, it seemed, killed too many people nowadays. Colton put his arm around John, his hand clutching his shoulder. Jennifer wiped her nose on her fist and walked over to her friends. She leaned on Colton and he put his other arm around her.

"Can I have a beer with you?" Marcy said, walking into the full light of the fire.

The three shifted on the log, staring at each other and at her, as if they were testing to see if this were a trap. Jennifer pulled a can from the bag and handed it over.

Marcy took it and sat at the far end of the log.

"Tell me about your friend," she said.

———

She could only finish half her drink before she decided to leave the gang. If she had finished the whole thing, she would have wanted to stay, but the night was for them and their grief, not hers. Marcy leaned over the concrete barrier of Bucky's Bridge, and in the still darkness, she heard the tail end of a story, something about where they would hang the paintings. The shadows of the gang hovered around the edges of the firelight as thick clouds of smoke folded over the river like a rotten fog. *A place like this*, Marcy thought. The gang was right about dying, about there being better places to do it. She set the trash bag onto the street and let her shoulders relax. But what about living? An owl called from some hall deep in the woods downriver and she thought of Levon, missing how he'd tried to hoot back. Owls didn't eat birdseed, but in the revolutions of these animals living and dying, Marcy let herself believe that some part of her husband was alive out there that night with her, with the gang below the bridge. Maybe, like Levon with the birds, some part of Leah had mingled with the fish in the Cass River. Maybe, too, an eagle or hawk had feasted on those fish from a river known to be calm but still powerful enough to show humanity who was boss. Maybe Leah was only a couple revolutions of life and death away from flying to freedom.

"Let's stay here until morning," Jennifer said, "then never come back."

Acknowledgments

I write because I read, and I read because Lila and Scott Deeren would read to me and Janel Deeren. Gretchen Comcowich, Sherri Hoffman, Kenny Kelly, Lauren Kelly, John Maloney, J. Ryan Sommers, Travis Tessmer, and Michael Welch are the best readers a writer could have; these stories reflect their generous time and attention. Sandi and Larry Novotny, Stacey Babcock, and Jean and Ben Harwood read, called, questioned, and supported year in and out. Jessica Johnston and Marzipan the Cat have graciously listened to me read and reread drafts; thanks for coming along for the journey.

C. Vince Samarco pointed me in the right direction. The late-too-soon but forever brilliant Samuel Park showed me I was on my way. Stephen Asma brought the monsters and votes of confidence. Aleksandar Hemon saw the first version of this book and helped make it better. John Freeman opened more doors than I probably know about.

There's not enough room to say how grateful I am to my agent, Justin Brouckaert, for his enthusiasm with this book over the years. That enthusiasm was shared by Marie Sweetman and the rest of the team at Wayne State University Press: Kelsey Giffin, Carrie Downes Teefey, Traci Cothran, Stephanie Williams, and Emily Gauronskas. Jen Anderson's copy edits were the polish I needed.

My writing life is fuller because of Peter Burzyński, Jenny Gropp, Alexa Nutile, Marla Sanvick, Laura Solomon, Michael Wendt, and every artist who came to Woodland Pattern Book Center in Milwaukee, Wisconsin. Liam Callanan, Bonnie Jo Campbell, Meredith Counts, Bryan Hurt, Mitch James, Mauricio Kilwein-Guevara, Valerie Laken, Patty McNair, Jeff Pfaller, Robert James Russell, Karen Tucker, and Larry Watson are brilliant editors, teachers, fellow writers, and trail guides.

Highest praise and acknowledgment to the anthologies and magazines that originally published versions of these stories. "The Mirror" and "Getting Out" appear in *Great Lakes Review*; "Bridge Work" appears in *Bartleby Snopes*; "Enough to Lose" is anthologized in *Tales of Two Americas: Stories of Inequality in a Divided Nation*; "The Run" appears in *Midwestern Gothic*; "Her, Guts and All" appears in *Joyland*.

These stories are fictional but my hometown that inspired them, Caro, Michigan, is as real as can be; I couldn't think of a better place to start from.